STUCK

STUCK

Diane Windsor

Published by Motina Books, LLC

Stuck

Published by Motina Books, LLC, Van Alstyne, Texas
www.MotinaBooks.com

Library of Congress Control Number: 2020946881
 Windsor, Diane
 Stuck

ISBN-13: 978-1-945060-20-5 (ebook)
ISBN-13: 978-1-945060-21-2 (paperback)

Dedication

This book is dedicated to all the families who spend countless hours in the hospital with their children who are battling cancer. When a child is diagnosed with cancer, time stops. Everything changes. "Normal" is a foreign word.

Then, even after treatment is over, childhood cancer is something that our kids will need to deal with for the rest of their lives.

Also, to the children who lost their very courageous battles and left us far too soon—Ryan, Gage, Connor, Myra, Jacob, Jacob, Ruby, Norah, Gabriella. We'll never forget you.

Chapter One

I take in a slow, deep breath. Then another. The sun feels so warm on my back. My eyes are closed and my body is relaxed. I crouch down in a ready stance, waiting for the sound of the starter pistol. I feel completely alone; I am completely within myself. I hear no chatter from the bleachers, no other runners on either side of me. Just me. The sun is shining; a very slight breeze blows from the south. It's a perfect morning to run. To race.

"Bam!" The shot rings out. I kick off the block, pumping my arms and legs as hard as possible. My dark ponytail streams behind me. All I can see are the stripes that border my lane through my peripheral vision. I always make sure that my feet are exactly where they are supposed to be. They never stray. Once, when I was just starting to race, I had been a bit over-confident during a competition. My gaze traveled upward, toward the sky, and I lost perspective. I remember wandering into the next lane, and there was a huge crash. I had collided with the runner next to me, and we ended up on the ground, a jumble of arms and legs. I was more embarrassed than I'd ever been, and now I make sure that never happens again.

Once around the quarter-mile lap. Then twice. I know not to push too hard right at the beginning. I'm in the middle of the pack, ready to push forward when the time comes. It isn't quite time yet, but it will be soon. Lap three is coming up, and that's when I decide to take a look around. Some of the girls have fallen behind; I'm not too surprised. Hold strong and steady, then kick it at the end. Too many of my teammates and competitors give it their all much too soon. I pass the marker for the final lap. It's time.

I kick it into high gear—my arms and legs are flying. Nothing matters more than crossing that finish line. And I do! I make it across! Right behind my girl, Angela Gutiérrez, aka "Speedy Gutiérrez."

We fall into each other's arms, laughing. We're going to the State Finals, thanks to Angie!

"I try so hard to kick your butt! I really try!" I tell my best friend. "But I just can't do it! I can't!"

"I'm sorry, Cassidy!" Angie replies, breathless. "Should I let you win once in a while?"

I grasp Angie's shoulders tightly and force her to look into my eyes.

"Never!" I say. "You do your best, every single time! I don't care who you're competing against!"

The Texas sun is shining brightly, and the temperature is so pleasant on this mid-October Saturday afternoon. Nothing like the oven-heat of a Texas summer. October is the best time of year in Texas.

We're starting to think about Halloween costumes. The year before we went as Jack and Rebecca Pearson, from *This Is Us*. I was Jack and I totally rocked the mustache. We have a few ideas for this year, but haven't been able to decide on anything yet. Maybe *Bob's Burgers*. We know that we need to get a move on; Halloween will be here before we knew it.

We walk together toward the locker room, to shower and change into non-sweaty clothes. There's a party tonight and I'm trying to talk Angie into coming with me.

Angie and I have been besties since fourth grade, when Angie moved from Los Angeles to the very suburban neighborhood where I was born. It was tough for Angie, a first generation Mexican-American, to fit in with the mostly white students in Cottonwood Bend. It's a neighborhood about fifteen miles north of Dallas; the streets are quiet and every front yard has a Bradford pear tree.

I remember when I first noticed Angie at school. No one was outright mean to her, but they weren't overly friendly, either. During morning recess she was sitting by herself watching all the other children play, talk, and be part of something that she wasn't.

Angie had been busy being sad and feeling sorry for herself, when I stuck a chocolate chip cookie in front of her face.

"Do you want one?" I asked her. I sat down next to her and said, "My mom put two in my lunch, and I'm full."

After that, we were always together. Chocolate chip cookies are magical like that.

Angie's parents were born in Mexico and immigrated to the United States where she was born.

3

They spent several years in Los Angeles and decided to move to Texas when her father was able to get an entry-level position at Texas Instruments. The job provided excellent benefits and growth potential.

But Angie, of course, hated leaving the only home she'd ever known. She dreaded attending a new school and the thought of meeting new people scared her to death. Meeting me on that first day changed all of that.

We're juniors now, starting to think about what happens after high school. We both started running track two years ago, and we found out we are pretty good, especially Angie. There are scholarship opportunities for her. I'm not good enough for scholarships, but I really get a charge out of racing. And, when Angie isn't racing, I do have a halfway decent chance of winning. Most importantly, I like running with Angie. We have fun together, and always support each other.

Don't think I resent her for being so good. I don't, not for a minute. I really want Angie to get a full scholarship at a great university. I'll probably go to community college for the first couple of years, then transfer to a university. But Angie's got the stuff to be a superstar.

"Are you going to Sam's party tonight?" I ask her. Both of us just showered and we're pulling on our clean clothes.

"I wanted to, but this race kinda took it out of me. I think I'll just hang out at home tonight."

"Really?" That's a surprise. We've been talking about this party for days. "But Connor is supposed to be there."

"I know. I really wanted to go, but I feel kinda crappy right now. I might have pushed myself too hard.

4

I'm sorry."

"Geez, Angie, you don't have to be sorry! Should I stay with you tonight? We can hang out at your house and eat your mom's salsa verde."

"Oh no, you go to the party. I don't think I'll be much fun tonight. I want to sleep for a while and then just veg later on." Angie turns her back to me, reaching for her jeans from the locker.

I'm still facing in her direction as she turns. What I see causes me to gasp loudly.

"What the hell did you do to the back of your legs?" I exclaim. I'm louder than I probably should be. My voice echoes through the empty locker room.

Angie cranes her neck to get a better look. "It's hard for me to see. What is it?"

"You have some serious bruises on the back of your thighs. Go look in the full-length mirror by the sinks. It might be easier for you to see over there. Come on."

We walk over to the sink area where there's a large mirror. It's at the end of the row of five sinks, mounted against the stark white tile. Angie, dressed only in a t-shirt and panties, stands in front of the mirror at an angle that allows the best view of the backs of her legs.

She just stares at her reflection; she doesn't say a word. Against her olive skin are bruises that are so dark, they look almost black. Angie looks shocked. The bruises are enormous. They cover almost the entire backs of her thighs. There are even some small ones on her calves. How has she not noticed this before?

"Does it hurt?" I ask. The dark splotches look like they're very painful.

"I don't know." Angie bent down and gingerly touches a dark spot. She says that it's tender and sore, but not excruciating. "Do you think it's from running?" she asks.

"I guess it could be, but I've never seen anything like it. It looks like someone's been beating you."

She stops speaking and looks at me.

"Oh, knock it off Cass. Nobody's touched me. I have no idea what this is."

"You should go to the doctor," I tell her.

She shakes her head at me. "Oh, I don't think so. I'm sure it'll just get better after a while."

I make a face at her, furrowing my brow, and make a kind of smirk with my mouth. I think she's full of crap.

"Angie, you need to have that looked at. Come on, I can take you to Urgent Care right now."

"Right now? But it's Saturday afternoon! You have that party tonight!"

"If it isn't a big deal then it won't take long. Let's just stop by."

"If I call my mother and tell her I'm going to Urgent Care, she's gonna freak out."

"We don't have to tell her. It's probably nothing, like you said. We only need to tell her if it's something she needs to know about." I'm trying to sound reassuring. "Which she won't. She won't need to know because it'll be fine."

"Oh, all right. If it'll get you to shut up you can take me to freaking Urgent Care. Just let me put my pants on."

Chapter Two

Urgent Care centers and stand-alone Emergency Rooms are as common as McDonald's in any suburb across America; my suburb is no different. It isn't unusual to see two of them on the same block. They're everywhere! It reminds me of how McDonald's and Burger King restaurants are often in the same parking lot.

I pull my light blue, ten-year-old Camry (her name is Elsa) into the parking lot of the closest one. The letters E and R are big and red above the front doors.

"Do you have your insurance card with you?" I ask Angie, as I pull the key out of the ignition and open my door.

"Yeah, I think it's in my wallet."

We both climb out of the car. Angie is nervous; she thinks this visit is overkill, but I can tell that part of her is wondering if there could be something wrong with her. It better not mess with her running. She knows that she'll have to start applying for athletic scholarships soon. Running will pay for her college. Her parents don't have any money saved for her education—that will be all on her. She doesn't mind, though. She feels that since she's the one wanting to go to college, she should be the one paying for it. Her parents have other things to worry about.

One thing Angie is certain about is that she absolutely will not take out student loans. She plans to work part-time while she attends school, apply for scholarships, and, hopefully, get some athletic scholarship money, too.

She has it all planned out.

I lead the way into the waiting room. It isn't too busy on this early Saturday afternoon. Hopefully, they won't make us wait very long. A large flat-screen on one wall is playing a popular home improvement show. This one features the two hunky brothers who renovate homes for families. Most of the people who are waiting their turn seem to be enthralled by the hand-scraped wood flooring and shiplap.

There's also a play area along one wall. A little girl is playing with Legos on a table. Her mother sits nearby, looking at something fascinating on her phone.

There are two employees at the reception desk. Both are busily typing away on their computers. It takes a moment before one of them looks up and notices us standing there.

I'm starting to get pretty annoyed. The word "urgent" is in the name of their business. These people are supposed to be helpful. How much longer do we need to wait?

Just when I open my mouth to say something, the

young, blonde woman looks up with a smile.

"Can I help you?"

"I have some bruises on the back of my legs," Angie told her. "My overly-anxious friend here said I should have them looked at." She gave the worrywart some serious side-eye.

"Do you have insurance?"

Angie opens her wallet and hands the card across the desk.

The woman's fingers fly over the keys as she types all of the information into the computer. Suddenly, she stopped. She looks at Angie and asks, "You're only sixteen? Do your parents know you're here?"

"Sure. My mom's at work, and she told me to come on over." Good girl! You're pretty good at fibbing! "Also, I think I have a parental consent document on file with you."

Angie, like me, often visited Urgent Care on her own, for our annual sports physicals. As long as they had parental consent in their system, it was fine for us to show up on our own.

"Okay then. Take this form and fill it out for me. It's been a while since you've been here, and we need to make sure that all your information is current. You're looking at about a thirty minute wait right now."

Angie takes the clipboard from the woman's hand. We make our way over to a couple of seats that have a good view of the hot brothers on TV. Angie flips the pages as she scans the questions on the sheets.

"Geez, I have to go way back to get all this family history. I don't know half of this crap."

"Just write down what you know," I suggest. OMG, I am loving these barn doors that slide across the wall on cast iron tracks. "I'm gonna live in a house with doors like that someday."

Angie is concentrating on completing the forms. She really doesn't know much about her family's health history. She hasn't seen any of her grandparents since she was tiny; she isn't even sure if any of them are still alive. Her dad is a little overweight, but she doesn't know if he has high blood pressure or cholesterol. What about diabetes? Is there insulin in her house?

"Ugh! This is too much! Okay, I'll just fill in what I know." She's finished in two minutes.

"Angie Gutiérrez!"

We both stand up at the same time. A door is held open by a smiling medical assistant.

"I didn't know the answers to all of these questions," Angie tells the woman as she hands her the clipboard.

"It's okay, honey. We'll just go with what you wrote down."

"Do you want me to come?" I ask.

"Hell yeah!" Angie grabs my hand and drags me through the door.

During the next few minutes, Angie is instructed to pee in a cup and blood is drawn from her veins. She ends up sitting on an exam table covered with a flimsy gown that is wide open in the back. I sit on a chair, reading a People magazine that's several months old.

"Hey, did you know that George Clooney and his wife had twins? That's so cool!" I always loved the Oceans movies.

"I think that happened last year," says Angie. "Hey, I need a magazine. Where's one for me?"

"This is the only one."

"Well then you need to talk to me. Why do we have

to wait so long in the exam room? We already waited in the waiting room. We shouldn't have to wait anymore!"

I'm about to make a snarky reply about how the patient needs to have patience, when the door opens. A man with shaggy strawberry blond hair and a neatly trimmed beard enters the exam room. This guy looks young—not much older than we are. His expression is hard to read; there's a small smile on his face, but it isn't reflected in his eyes.

"Hi there, Angie. I'm Dr. Tyrell."

"Hello."

"How are you feeling?"

"A little tired. And I have these weird bruises on the back of my legs that I just noticed."

"Right."

Dr. Tyrell exudes calmness. I can tell that he's trying to make Angie feel comfortable; I think it's working. He sits down on the wheelie-stool, so he's at the same eye-level as Angie.

"As you know, we took a blood sample from you today and we ran a CBC."

"What's that?" I ask. I've been sitting quietly in the other chair in the room, trying to figure out what's happening by studying the young doctor's face. I'm not too great at keeping my mouth shut when I have questions.

Dr. Tyrell smiles. "It's a Complete Blood Count. We check your hemoglobin, white blood cells, platelets, and a couple other things."

He gives me that same semi-smile and then looks directly at Angie.

"Angie, the results we have are preliminary. More tests need be run. But your white blood cell count indicates that you might have some form of leukemia or lymphoma."

Angie looks like she hasn't heard him correctly.

"Leukemia or lymphoma? Isn't that cancer?"

"Yes, it is. You'll need to go to the hospital straight from here. I've already called Children's to let them know you're coming."

"Wait, wait, wait," I interject. Finally, I'm able to form some words. Cancer? Angie doesn't have freaking cancer. "Doctor, this is ridiculous. Your test has to be wrong. Angie just won a race today, and she's going to compete at the State Finals in a couple of weeks."

"Acute forms of leukemia appear very quickly, out of the blue. Angie's white count was 200,000 per microliter. That's what is making me believe it's a form of blood cancer."

"What's the normal range for white cells?" asks Angie, in a very quiet voice.

"Around 10,000," replies the doctor. "I know this is a lot to take in. You'll have more answers and more information once you get to the hospital. You need to call your parents and let them know you're going to Children's."

"I'll call them," I say. "So, we should go now?"

"Yes, you should. Check in at the Emergency Room. They know you're coming."

Dr. Tyrell smiles at Angie again. This must be one of the most difficult parts of being a doctor–telling a young person, in the prime of her life, that everything is about to change. He turns the wheelie chair to look at me.

"I need you to be in charge right now, okay?"

I nod, even though I feel as shocked as I know

Angie is.

"When you get to the hospital and she's admitted to a room, one of the first people you meet will be the social worker. You might meet her today, or it could be tomorrow. But she'll be an important contact. Write down everything she says, or even use your phone to record it. She won't mind. You'll also need to take really good notes when you talk to the doctors. Can you do that?"

My voice is a bit shaky as I answer, "I can do that. I'll call her mom, too, and let her know what's happening."

He smiles warmly at me.

"Good job. Why don't you and I step outside? That'll give Angie a chance to get dressed, and you can call her mother."

He opens the door to the examination room and gestures to me to lead the way. With a kind look over his shoulder, he says to Angie, "We'll see you in a couple minutes. Take your time."

I pull my phone out of my pocket and dial Mrs. Gutiérrez's number. I am not looking forward to this conversation.

I notice the door open behind me and Angie steps out, pulling on her sweatshirt.

"Oh, she just came out of the room, Mrs. Gutiérrez."

I hand Angie the phone.

"Talk to your mom," I tell her. "She's freaking out a little."

Angie sighs. Of course she is.

"Hi Mama," she says into my iPhone. "No, I don't have any other information than what Cassidy already told you. We're going to Children's Hospital now. You can meet us there."

She holds the phone away from her ear and scowls. Through the speaker I can hear the sound of a very anxious mother speaking Spanish very quickly.

"Mama, just meet us there, and we can start figuring this out. Who knows, they might not even be right about this. How can I have leukemia or lymphoma? That's crazy. Okay. I know. Yes, in Dallas. I'll see you there. Love you, too."

She hands the phone back to me. "I guess we should go."

Chapter Three

Angie uses the phone to navigate to Children's while I drive. Luckily it's a Saturday and there isn't much traffic. If it had been a weekday, the drive would have been a nightmare. The sun shines brightly through the windshield, and the soothing voices of NPR come through the speakers.

"I don't even have a toothbrush with me," Angie says, thoughtfully.

"I think they'll have one for you there." I turn on the blinker to make a left turn into the hospital's entrance. There are plenty of signs that point to the Emergency Room, so it isn't hard to find.

"But I don't have anything! I don't have my phone charger, or laptop. What about a change of clothes? Or a hairbrush?" The pitch of her voice is getting higher; she sounds kind of frantic.

Cars are all around us, trying to either pull into a

parking garage or park on the street. Even so, I wind my way around to the patient drop-off area. I put the car in park and turn to face Angie.

"I don't want you to worry about any of that. I will go get you anything you need. Really! I'll drive home and get your own stuff, or I can run to that Kroger we passed. Let's just go inside, okay?"

Angie nods but she doesn't look very reassured. She probably doesn't know what to think.

We drive into the covered parking garage next to the Emergency Room entrance. There are signs everywhere, pointing the way to various departments. We walk through a walkway encased in glass; on either side are play areas and flower gardens. Angie tells me that she thinks it looks very pretty and happy. Nothing bad can happen in a place that looks so full of life.

The ER entrance comes into view. Just as we are about to walk through the double-doors, a slight woman with shoulder-length black hair begins running toward us.

"Angie! Cassidy! Did you just get here? What's happening?" Rosa Gutiérrez throws her arms around her daughter.

"We just got here, Mama. We haven't gone inside yet."

"Okay." She takes her daughter's arm protectively, as if she's preparing to do battle. "Let's go in."

"Hi there! How can we help you today?" the receptionist is extremely friendly and chipper. Angie is checked in quickly, since Dr. Tyrell had called ahead with her information.

"Can I see your insurance information, ho-ney?" Angie hands her the card.

"Mama," the receptionist says to Mrs. Gutiérrez,

"are you the policy holder?"

"No, it's through my husband's employer."

"Okay, great. Please have a seat in the waiting area, and we'll be with you as soon as possible." She gestures toward the rows of uncomfortable plastic chairs.

The three of us have just sat down and prepared ourselves for a long wait (it's the Emergency Room, after all) when a door opens and a nurse with short, curly red hair calls Angie's name.

We all stand and walk toward the door.

"Hi sweetheart! My name is Sue. We have a room all ready for you." Sue is super-sweet. She keeps smiling and chatting as she leads us to the elevator bank.

"Where are we going?" I ask her.

"Up to the sixth floor, honey."

"Is Angie being admitted to the hospital?" asks Mrs. Gutiérrez.

"Yes, she is. We need to find out what's going on and the best way to treat her."

"How long will she be here?"

"Ma'am, I'm afraid we don't know that yet. The doctors will be running tests over the next day or two. But this is the best place for her. We'll take excellent care of her."

The elevator opens onto a bright hallway. Murals of flowers and jungle animals are painted on the walls. There's even a small exercise room. I see a treadmill, an elliptical, and windows that look out over the city.

Sue places her ID badge against the sensor, and the doors open automatically. We pass a nurses' station where several hospital employees stand talking. She opens the door of room 51.

"Here we are!" she trills cheerfully.

STUCK

A large pane of glass in the middle of the door is painted with a scene from Disney's *Beauty and the Beast*. Chip and Mrs. Potts gaze at each other adoringly.

Angie, her mom, and I walk into the room.

"Angie, the doctor will be in soon to talk to you. You can make yourself comfortable in the meantime."

She closes the door behind her as she walks out, leaving us alone.

"It's a nice room," I say. I'm looking all around, trying to figure out if Angie will like it. The room is filled with natural light streaming in from a window that takes up the entire wall. The bed is in the center of the room, with the head close to all kinds of machines and valves.

"Will those be used on me?" Angie asks. Neither her mom or I answer. We don't really want to think about it.

On the wall across from the bed a large TV is mounted on the wall. A dorm-sized refrigerator is nestled beneath a counter-top. I open the fridge door to check out the stash, but it's empty. I think there should be some apple juice in there, at least.

I continue my tour of the room; I poke my head in the bathroom. The toilet paper looks rough and uncomfortable. I'll have to bring some Charmin.

On the stand next to the bed lies a menu.

"Hey, are you hungry?" I ask Angie. "We can order some food."

"Yeah, I am a little. Let's see what they have."

"You can't go wrong with quesadillas."

"All righty, call 'em up."

Mrs. Gutiérrez is seated in the arm-chair next to the bed. Angie is sitting on the wide window sill, gazing out at the city below. Her face is bathed in the sunlight.

She glances at her mother, sitting in that big chair all alone. There is definitely room for one more. Angie stands and moves to sit on her mama's lap, like I haven't seen her do in many years. She curls up tight, laying her head on her chest.

Of course, just as she gets comfy the door opens. It isn't the quesadillas, but another nurse. Her hands are full of items encased in plastic. She means business.

"Hello, ladies. Where's our guest of honor?"

Angie untangles herself from her mom's lap and stands up.

"That's me."

"Hi, Angie, I'm Kristin. I'll be taking care of you tonight. The doctor will see you soon, but I'll get you started with an IV."

"Okay," Angie's voice shakes a bit as she replies.

"Do you want to change into something a little more comfortable? I don't have PJs for you, but I can get you a gown."

"Um, all right."

Kristin pulls a hospital gown from a nearby cupboard and hands it to her.

"Go ahead and change, sweetheart. Then hop into bed."

Angie walks into the bathroom to change. She comes out a minute later wearing the gown and carrying her jeans, t-shirt, and running shoes. She still wears her socks.

"Hop up, honey, and we'll get started."

I'm cringing as Kristin starts working at putting the IV in Angie's arm. Geez, I hate needles of all kinds. It doesn't matter that I'm not the one being the one stuck—I just hate seeing it go in. It doesn't seem to bother Angie much. The nurse gave her a little bit of a local anesthetic first, so that probably helps.

"One of the perks of being in a children's hospital is that we can give you that local to make it easier for you," she tells us.

The door opens, and a petite brunette enters the room.

"Hello, Angie. I'm Dr. Monahan. You can call me Kate." Kate has a warm smile and really cool Ray-Ban glasses. She is wearing an awesome brown and pink polka-dot dress.

"I like your dress," Angie says.

"Thanks. The coolest thing, is that it has pockets!" Kate demonstrates. She sways her hips a little bit, causing the skirt to twirl. She is adorable.

Kate turns toward Mrs. Gutiérrez. "You're Mom?" she asks.

Mrs. Gutiérrez nods.

"And are you Sister?" she asks me.

"I'm her best friend."

"Oh, it's great that you're here. Mom, do I have permission to speak freely in front of everyone?"

Mrs. Gutiérrez nods again.

"Excellent. Here's what we know so far. With a white count at 200,000 per microliter, we know that you have some type of blood cancer. Now we need to figure out what kind, so we can treat it the right way."

I'm thinking about what Dr. Tyrell had said about being the one to capture all of the information that the doctors will tell us. I grab my backpack and rummage around until I find a fairly clean notebook.

"What's a microliter?" I ask the doctor.

"That's a great question. A microliter is one-millionth of a liter. A drop of blood is made up of approximately sixty microliters."

I'm writing furiously in my notebook, trying to grab all of the details. I figure that we might not need all of the info, but having too much can't hurt, right?

"And what's the normal amount of white cells? I think the doctor at Urgent Care said it's around 10,000. Is that right?" I ask.

"That's right! It can actually be between 10,000 and 15,000. Your white blood cells are the infection fighters. If you have a very serious infection and you end up in the ICU, your white count is probably around 25,000. That's how we know that we're dealing with blood cancer, because your counts are off the charts."

She pauses to look at Angie and her mother. They're both listening attentively, although Kate doesn't seem to be completely sure how much is being absorbed. My guess is that it's good that a non-family member is there. I'm really trying to stay on top of things. My friend and her mom must feel like they're drinking from a fire hose.

"It's your bone marrow that produces all of your blood cells," Kate continues. "Red, white, and platelets all come from there. Your bone marrow is also producing the abnormal cells. So, first thing tomorrow morning we're going to do a bone marrow biopsy. You'll be fast asleep during this procedure, so it won't hurt. You'll be a bit sore afterward, but we'll manage that pain for you. During the procedure, we're going to drill a tiny hole through your hip bone and remove some of the bone marrow. Then we'll analyze it and be able to see exactly what kind of cancer you have."

"How long will all of this take? I want to go home and back to school," Angie says.

"That's a great question. I'm afraid it's going to

take some time. Your plans will need to be put on hold for a little while. We have Child Life specialists on staff who will help you progress with your schoolwork, and I'm sure Cassidy will bring you anything you need to work on. But for now, getting you healthy is the number one priority."

I nod my head.

"I'll help, Angie," I assure her.

Doctor Monahan continues, "While we're not yet sure what kind of blood cancer you have, I can give you an idea of what treatment will look like. There will be chemo—probably a lot of it. Treatment will take the better part of a year, maybe longer. You'll have to be strong, Angie. You'll have to fight. I don't know you yet, but I know that you're a runner. You're a winner. I believe that you can beat this. But it doesn't matter what I think. It matters what you think. Can you beat this?"

Angie looks at her mother and then at me. She knows what we both want to hear. We want her to say that sure, of course she's going to beat this. That she will fight and have a wonderful, positive attitude through the whole thing. But she isn't sure that it will all work out. How can she be? This is cancer—the big C. Saying that to her friends and family won't help, will it? She'll tell us what we want to hear and hope it's the truth.

"Yes," she tells all of us. "I can beat this. I will definitely beat this."

Kate smiles. "Good. That's what I want to hear."

With excellent timing, the quesadilla arrives.

"Looks like it's dinner time," says Kate. "On that note, I'm going to let you get settled. I'll see you tomorrow."

Chapter Four

Six Months Earlier

Our junior year was almost over, and we were not feeling school anymore. Both Angie and I just wanted to be anywhere else. The track season had ended, so our time after school was completely our own. We were blissfully enjoying the sunny April afternoon, wishing that Elsa was a convertible. Driving around with the top down would have been sublime.

We were both wearing shorts a little prematurely—it was April, and while there had already been a few days in the low-80s, there was always the chance of clouds, rain, and chilly weather. We didn't care. We had on matching blue jean cutoffs (thank you, TJ Maxx) and tie-dyed t-shirts. No, we didn't go to school like that today. We just changed clothes as soon as we could after school.

STUCK

I pulled into the parking lot of our local Dollar Tree. Angie and I could easily spend hours there, finding the treasures that a lot of people often miss. Most people run in for a birthday card, bouquet of balloons, or maybe a set of cheap glassware, but not us.

The double doors slid open before us. Angie made a beeline for the seasonal items, and I went to office supplies. Instead of browsing the middle shelf like most people, I got on my hands and knees and dug around the bottom shelf. That's where all the good stuff was, that nobody else found. I loved the office supply section because of the adorable little organizing boxes and baskets.

And, jackpot! Stuffed in the back of the bottom shelf, behind a pile of torn up spiral notebooks, I found four packages of flamingo-shaped string lights. I was madly in love with string lights. Sure, I needed to buy my own batteries, but I would do anything for the twinkly, sparkling lights. At Christmas time they were shaped like snowflakes, and in the fall, they looked like tiny maple leaves.

We met at the front and compared our individual hauls.

"Ooooo," Angie said admiringly. "I love the lights!"

"Me too! We need to decorate Elsa with them. What did you find?"

She held out her hand to show me a pile of multi-colored kazoos.

"We can prank people with these!"

"Prank? What are you talking about?"

"You'll see."

On the way to the check-out I grabbed a couple packs of Double-A batteries so I could fire up my string lights right away. Back in the car I popped the batteries into the cases of the lights and wound them around the rear-view mirror and the visors. I flipped the switches, and a very faint, pink light shone around the edges of the windshield. It wasn't as bright as I had hoped it would be. It would be better at night.

I pulled out of the parking lot, wondering where we should go now.

"Wanna go to Sonic?" I asked Angie. I was in the mood for fried mozzarella sticks—I was always in the mood for fried mozzarella sticks.

"Yes, please!"

Sonic was only about a half mile away, so it would take us practically no time to get there. There were a few stoplights along our path, and the first one we came to was red.

All of a sudden, I heard a high-pitched whine coming from the passenger seat. I turned to face Angie, and I saw that she was blowing hard into one of her new kazoos. Her cheeks were puffed out and her eyes were scrunched shut.

Then she stopped and looked out the passenger window, which was rolled all the way down. The people in the car next to her were looking around, trying to figure out where the sound was coming from. I looked out my window and saw the same thing.

"Look around like you don't know where it's coming from!" Angie said, as she tried to suppress her giggles.

I did as I was told and looked behind me and to my left and right, as if I were looking for something I couldn't find. Angie blew air into that stupid plastic tube again. I saw that she was hunched over in her seat, so she was nearly invisible. Then she popped up and looked all around her, just like the people in the cars next to us, wondering where that ridiculous noise was coming from.

"This is your brilliant prank?" I asked her, with disbelief. I started laughing just because it was so dorky.

"Hey, it was funny! They didn't know where the noise was coming from!"

"Oh, okay, if you say so. It was funny." She punched me in the shoulder.

The light turned green, and I was cracking up as I stepped on the gas and headed toward Sonic.

Chapter Five

It's pushing midnight by the time I get home from the hospital. I walk through the front door, carrying the duffle that is packed with my running clothes from earlier that day. Was that just this afternoon? Geez, it seems like days ago.

My mom is still awake. The glow from the TV softly illuminates the family room.

"Hi, honey." Mom stands up to give me a hug. Our nine-year-old Heinz-57 pup, Brandy, is right at Mom's heels, like always. Mom's little shadow.

She places her mug of tea on the coffee table, mutes the TV, and wraps her arms around me. I breathe in her scent of patchouli and jasmine. Even though I'm about six inches taller than my five-foot-two-inch tall mom, I bend my head to rest it on her shoulder. I don't think I'll ever be too old to need my mom. Mom lets me go, so I crouch down to give

Brandy some love, too.

"How's Angie doing, honey?"

"Okay for now. They're going to do a biopsy tomorrow to figure out exactly what kind of blood cancer she has. Then they'll come up with a detailed treatment plan. They seem to think it's leukemia."

Mom pats my back gently, just like when I was five. It's so comforting.

"Oh, that's just awful," she says. "I'm so thankful that you're okay. This is why I never had you vaccinated. This is the kind of damage that vaccines can cause."

I lift my head and look at her.

"Really?" I ask. "But the last time Angie was vaccinated was when she was little. You think that caused her leukemia?"

"The toxins from vaccines stay in your system forever. They cause damage for the rest of your life."

Mom picks up her mug and takes a sip of tea.

"And, think about it this way. She was vaccinated and came down with cancer. You don't have any vaccinations, and you don't have cancer. It makes total sense. I've always known what's best for you, doll-face."

She stands up on her tip-toes to kiss my doll-face on my forehead.

"I'm tired, sweetie. Good night."

"Night, Mom. Oh, hey, wait a minute."

She's already halfway up the staircase, Brandy right behind her, and turns back to look at me.

"I'll be at the hospital most of tomorrow. They're doing some procedures, and I want to be there for Angie."

"Okay, that's fine. Just don't let anybody vaccinate

you while you're there," she jokes.

"Sure, Mom, no prob."

My mom has always been what some people called "crunchy." She eats only organic vegetables, believes in the healing power of essential oils, and doesn't trust modern medicine—much. There was the time when I was eight and I broke my arm when I fell off the monkey bars at the playground. My mom had rushed me to the emergency room to have the bone set. I also remember a few follow-up visits with a pediatric orthopedic doctor, until the cast came off. But that was it. I can't recall going to the doctor for any kind of regular check-ups or physicals. When school required a sports physical so I could compete in track, I just went to Urgent Care.

Mom is a fan of herbal supplements and acupuncture. She believes in the power of all things natural. I always thought that was fine, of course. If she believes these things work for her, then that's great.

Every morning she fixes a super-fruit smoothie for the two of us. Mom always adds supplements that boost my brain functions and give me extra energy for my day. I'm not sure if any of this worked, but the smoothies are tasty and keep me full until lunch.

I've never had a second thought about Mom's thoughts about health and wellness. I get sick occasionally, of course, but everyone does. And, when I do, my mom takes care of me by reducing the fever with cold cloths and lukewarm baths. She also makes me drink a tea heavy with turmeric. Not the powder, either. She buys the fresh root from an Asian grocery store and steeps the orange shreds in hot water for a long time. Then she adds cayenne pepper for that extra zing. It is *nasty*.

But I choke it down because Mom promises that it will strengthen my immune system and help me heal quickly. And, because my mother tells me to.

I have a vivid memory of coming down with the chicken pox when I was in second grade. I was kept out of school for almost two weeks. Mom had me take oatmeal baths to relieve the itching, but it was a losing battle. It was the most miserable time of my life. There were even blisters inside my mouth that made eating complete agony. It was horrible.

I remember finally returning to school after the whole ordeal. I was sitting in the cafeteria eating lunch with a few other little girls.

"Why did you get the chicken pops?" one of them asked.

"I don't know. I just did."

"My mommy said that I'll never get the chicken pops because the doctor gave me a shot when I was little," piped up another.

"That's what my mommy said, too," said another. "Didn't the doctor give you the shot?"

I wasn't sure what to say. I kind of knew about my mother's anti-medical views from a very early age. Even as a second grader I knew that Mom would not take me to the doctor unless she didn't see any other alternative. But for some reason I couldn't explain, I didn't want to admit this to my friends.

"I think I got the shot. Maybe it didn't work for me." I concentrated on eating my peanut butter sandwich and apple slices, wishing that a doctor had given me a shot when I was little, if it would have prevented the itchy misery of chicken pops.

I make my way to my room, thinking about that memory. My dad hadn't been around much during that time of my life. He and my mother had divorced when I was very small. I don't get to spend as much time with him as I would have liked; my parents don't get along very well. But Dad and I have dinner together once a week, and whenever I want to talk, he's there for me.

I look at the time on my phone—a quarter past midnight. He's a night owl, so he's probably still up. I text him first, just to make sure.

Are you up? No big deal if you're not. Not a 911— I type.

His reply comes almost instantaneously.

I'm awake. What's up? Wanna call?

I dial my dad's number and flop down on the bed.

"What's up, pumpkin?" he asks as he answers the phone. My dad, Mark Coleman, is my best friend. Well, next to Angie. He's an accountant who owns his own business. He helps people with their taxes and gets them set up with QuickBooks software. Fascinating stuff like that.

"Hey, Dad. I got some bad news today."

"What happened?" He sounds anxious.

"It's not me, I'm fine. It's Angie. She's in the hospital. They think she has leukemia."

"Crap, honey, that really stinks. I'm sorry."

"Yeah, me too. When I told Mom about it today, she said something that sounded a little weird."

"Okay…"

I laugh. "Why do you say it like that?"

"You know your mom and I don't agree on much, honey. But that's all right. What did she say?"

"She made a comment that vaccines cause leukemia. She said that's why Angie has it, and I don't."

There's silence on the other end of the cellular waves.

31

"Dad? Did I lose you?"

"No, I'm still here. I'm just trying to figure out how to say what I want to say without sounding like a jerk."

I don't really think that's possible. My dad's a great guy who never says anything bad about my mom. I was under two when they split up, so it isn't like I ever missed a home complete with two married parents. I never knew one.

While I love Mom very much, I always feel that it's easier to talk to Dad about the tough stuff. It's Dad who gave me *the* talk (you know the one) and he even took me shopping for my first bra. He never talks down to me, like I'm just his child—he treats me like an equal. I always thought it's because we don't live together. We share mutual respect because of who we are, and not because he's my dad and I'm his kid.

"I've never told you how your mom and I met, have I?"

"No, I don't think so."

"We were young and she knocked my socks off." I can hear the smile in his voice.

"We were so different. I was studying Economics at CU in Boulder, and she was this gorgeous flower child."

"A flower child?" I think that sounds pretty crazy. "In the 2000s?"

"Well, it was Boulder! She was pretty normal for Boulder. Her hair was so long. She wore these flowing skirts that touched the floor. Her spirit was so free. I've never known anyone who just lived in the moment like your mom. We did all kinds of things in the outdoors. Hiking, camping, and cross-country skiing in the winter. We didn't do downhill; she couldn't stand the crowds and the lift lines."

He pauses.

"And then she was expecting you. I wanted to get married, but she said that we didn't need a piece of paper to prove that we loved each other. You were delivered by a midwife in our apartment, which scared me to death. I kept thinking that something was going to go wrong and that we'd never make it to a hospital in time. I was sure I would lose one or both of you. But nothing happened. You were both fine.

"I'll never forget that day," he continues. "Beth was laboring on our bed, and she would get up occasionally to walk around. The midwife had said that would help move things along, but to me it felt like it was taking forever! She refused to take any drugs, of course."

I listen to this story without interrupting. This is my birth story, and I never heard it before. Well, that's not completely true. I never heard my dad's version of the story. Mom told me about her and the midwife, but there was nothing about my dad. This is fascinating.

"Your mom kept telling me that women had been doing this without drugs for centuries. She refused to take anything.

"I wasn't going to fight her, of course. But watching her go through this without being able to do anything made me feel completely helpless. Once in a while she let me rub her back, and I fed her ice chips, but that was it. You were born on the bed in the middle of our tiny studio apartment. It was smack dab in the middle of the combination living/dining room. We used to sit on the bed at night to read books or watch TV. Your mom would cook dinner every night, and we would listen to Van Morrison and the Grateful Dead. She always created something healthy; organic and vegetarian were her specialties." He pauses for a moment to sigh. "She was a master in the kitchen.

"I went to school during the day and worked part-time at Alfalfa's. That was a natural food store, like Whole Foods before there was a Whole Foods in every town. Every night I looked forward to getting home to your mom. We would talk and dance for hours in that cramped little space.

"Man, she was making so much noise when she was having you! She grunted and screamed so loud; I was so sure that something was very wrong. It took hours; the more time went on, the more agitated and worried I was. And then, all of a sudden, it was over! There you were, a pink, squirmy, little angel. You weren't even crying—your eyes were wide open and you were just taking everything in. It was incredible."

I'm still listening with full attention, just loving this story. Hearing my dad go on about that time in his life, I can practically see that teeny apartment and hear Van Morrison singing *Brown Eyed Girl*.

"We were so happy. I thought it would last forever, especially once you were born. You brought so much joy into our home. And you were safe and healthy! I was over the moon and madly in love with both of you. Everything was perfect; until it wasn't."

When he continues his story, I can hear a change in his voice. It had been so happy when he was talking about everything leading up to my birthday. Now, when he starts his story again, he suddenly sounds sad.

"A few days after you were born, I started talking to your mom about taking you to a pediatrician for a check-up. I was only nineteen, but I knew that a newborn baby needed some medical care. Your weight needed to be checked, other progress needed to be monitored, and I knew about vaccines, of course. I was vaccinated when I was a kid. But when I started talking about that, that's when all hell broke loose."

"Why, Dad? What do you mean?"

He sighs. "Cassie, honey, I don't want to say bad things about your mother. She loves you and only wants what's best for you."

"I know that. And I know that you love me, too. I just want to know the truth. This thing with Angie has me pretty shook up. I want to help her."

"I don't know if anything I have to tell you can help Angie. All I can tell you is that the problems between your mom and me happened because of her thing with doctors and medicine. She believed that there was a conspiracy between the government, the medical community, and big pharma."

"A conspiracy? What kind of conspiracy?"

"I'm not really sure."

"So, that's why you split up?"

"Yeah, that was why. We were so far apart on these issues. She ended up getting a lawyer to draw up a formal separation agreement. In the agreement it stated that she had the authority to make all medical decisions for you. And it was signed by a judge. There wasn't a damn thing I could do about it."

"Really? Even though you're my dad?"

"The court order is the deciding factor. Your mom made a strong case about what she thought was best for you. And, she had a good lawyer. If I go against that order, I could go to jail."

"Wow, Dad, that's crazy!"

"I know. I'm glad that you're healthy and haven't really needed to go to the doctor. Except that time you broke your arm, and your mom took you in for that."

He pauses briefly. "Honey, it's late and I'm pretty tired. Did I answer your questions?"

"Sure, Dad, thanks. I'll talk to you later,"and we hang up after a couple of I love yous.

I let it all sink in. This is brand new information. I never thought to question my mom's decisions about how she takes care of me. I always thought I was a pretty healthy person, and I just didn't need to go to the doctor very often.

I check my phone to see what time it is—one in the morning. I should probably get some sleep too, since I want to get to the hospital early the next morning. I turn off the vintage lamp on my nightstand and fall asleep thinking about Angie.

Chapter Six

I hand the cashier a twenty-dollar bill and thank her for the bag of pastries and coffees. I'm a few blocks away from the hospital and stopped to pick up some doughnuts and lattes for Angie and her parents. I drive to the main hospital entrance and maneuver into the parking garage. Of course, I have to take a ticket to park, because it's not free to park at this hospital. Whatever.

I enter through the main entrance this time, instead of the Emergency Room entrance, like we did the day before. The lobby is large, with natural light streaming in from several directions. It's actually very cheerful.

Everyone needs to check in at the front desk, show an ID, and wear a sticky name badge while they visit. I plaster my badge to my t-shirt and make my way to the bank of elevators that lead to Angie's floor.

STUCK

On the way to the elevators I pass by an atrium with beautiful butterflies hanging from the ceiling. They look like they're made from metal, and they're all painted with bright colors. The ceiling from which they hang is adorned with thousands of tiny LED lights. It looks like they're flying through a star-filled sky.

I ride the elevator to the sixth floor and easily find Angie's room. You can't miss the painting on the window. Balancing the coffees and bag of doughnuts in one hand, I knock softly with the other, then open the door and step inside. Angie is sitting up in her bed—her mom and dad are there, and so is a young woman with dark hair, a clipboard, and a golden retriever.

Everyone, including the golden retriever, turns to look at me as I walk in.

"I brought doughnuts!" I announce.

"Great!" says the young woman. She stands to shake my hand. "I'm Julie, one of the Child Life specialists here at the hospital. And this is Bonnie."

I'm always up for meeting a new dog, and Bonnie meets all of my expectations of being adorable and fluffy.

"Cassidy, Angie was telling me that you're her best friend, right?"

I glance at Angie and nod.

"That's great. My job is to help Angie have as much 'normal' in her life as possible, while she goes through her treatment. You're going to have to help me with that. I'll reach out to the principal and teachers at school. I'll need you to collect assignments and kinda be the messenger between the school and the hospital. Are you up for that?"

"Of course," I tell her. "I plan to come here right

after school anyway. I'll do whatever you need me to."

"Great!" she pulls a business card out of her pocket and hands it to me. "You call me whenever you need to, or if you have any questions. I was telling Angie and her parents that no one expects her to do schoolwork if she doesn't feel up to it. But if she wants to, we'll help her in any way that we can."

I had set the coffees and doughnuts down on the table when I came in the room and been immediately distracted by Bonnie. Now I pick up the bag of sugary goodness and hand it to Angie.

"I got your favorite—Bavarian cream filled with chocolate frosting." I reach into the bag to grab one for Angie and hand it to her.

Instead of taking it from me, she pushes my hand away.

"Dammit, I can't have one. They told me that I'm having a procedure soon, and I can't have anything to eat or drink."

I think it would be kind of crappy of me if I start digging into my apple fritter, so I put the bag back on the table. I drink my coffee, though. Mr. and Mrs. Gutiérrez are sitting on the couch by the window, looking at paperwork together. Mrs. Gutiérrez is making notes in a small notebook.

I'm not sure what to say to anyone. I want to say something to make things better, but I have no idea what that could possibly be.

Angie looks over at her parents. They notice her gaze and stop what they're doing.

"Honey, how are you feeling?" asks her mother. "Can I get you anything? Do you need the nurse?"

"No, Mama, I'm fine. Just keep doing what you're doing."

Angie scoots up a bit in her bed and leans over to me.

"This is driving me crazy," she says. "They're already treating me different, like I'm super-fragile, or something."

"Like you're what?"

"Super-fragile," Angie replies.

"Super-fragile-calla-listic-expialidocious?"

Angie looks at me for a moment with a blank look on her face. Then she starts cracking up.

"You're such a dork!" she says.

"I'm not a dork—you're a dork."

She lowers her voice and scoots even closer to me.

"Look," she whispers. "I don't want to be treated like I'm sick. I mean, I know that I am, but I don't want people to treat me like I am. Especially you."

"Oh, you don't need to worry about me. I'll treat you just like I always have. Like the dork that you are."

"At least I'm a fast dork, and I'll always be faster than you!"

We're both laughing when the door opens. Kate, the doctor we met yesterday, walks in followed by a nurse.

"Good morning, Angie!" Kate says brightly. She's wearing another very cute dress. "Today's a big day for you. We have three procedures scheduled, but we'll knock all of those out at one time. And you'll be fast asleep for the whole thing."

She looks at Mr. and Mrs. Gutiérrez; Angie's mom's is prepared to take notes—her pen is poised above the paper.

"Here's what's happening today. We're going to do a bone marrow biopsy and a lumbar puncture. That means we'll take a sample of bone marrow and spinal fluid and analyze them. This will tell us exactly what kind of cancer you have. We think it's leukemia, but we need to know exactly what kind. Sometimes, leukemia will enter the spinal column, so we need to see if it's there yet. That's why we're doing a lumbar puncture."

Kate pauses to look at Angie. "Do you have any questions?"

"Will it hurt?"

"You won't feel a thing while it's happening. You'll be fast asleep. You might be a little sore afterwards, but we'll help you with the pain."

"Okay."

"There's one more procedure we're going to perform while you're under the anesthesia. We will need to insert a catheter into your jugular vein in your neck. I know that sounds scary, but it really isn't that bad."

Angie's eyes are wide.

"A catheter in my neck? What's that for?" her voice is a little shaky, and I don't blame her. I wouldn't want anything stuck in my neck.

"You have so many white blood cells right now, that we need to physically take some of them out of your body," Kate explains. "If we start giving you chemo and killing all of those extra cells, they'll die, break open, and your kidneys won't be able to process the electrolytes that are released from the cells effectively, and it could cause organ damage. So, we're going to perform a procedure called apheresis. Your blood will be removed from your body through the catheter, run through a centrifuge machine, and spun around really fast. Your white cells will be separated from the rest of your blood. They'll be collected in a bag and discarded, and the remaining blood will return to your body. It takes a few hours, and a technician will monitor the entire procedure. We'll probably get that started later this afternoon."

"I'll be connected to a machine the whole time?"

"Yes, you will, but you can eat, or watch TV, or anything else from your bed."

"Okay….."

Kate smiles. "I know it's a whole lot to take in, honey. We have to act fast to get on top of the disease. If you're ever in any pain, you let us know and we'll help you. If you have any questions, just ask."

Angie nods. Before she can say anything else, the door opens and a young black woman dressed in scrubs walks into the room.

"I'm with Transport," she says. "I'm taking Angie Gutiérrez down to the procedure room."

"She's all yours!" says Kate, as she stands up. "Mom and Dad, you can go with them, and then they'll show you where the waiting area is."

"Mrs. Gutiérrez, take the coffees," I stand up and hand her the hot drinks. "And the doughnuts. I'll wait up here, if that's okay."

"Okay, Cassidy, thank you."

Angie's entire bed is wheeled out the door and down the hall. The group disappears through a set of double-doors that needs to be opened with a badge. I watch them all go through to the next hallway, then the doors close on them and I'm alone.

I decide to take a walk around and scope out the floor. The family lounge is just a smidge past Angie's room. It's nice, with comfy couches, a TV, and a Little Free Pantry. That's pretty cool—they don't even charge for the snacks. There's a sign written on a small chalkboard that reads, "Free for Families."

I open the fridge—there are mini cans of Sprite on one shelf and teeny tubs of apple sauce on another. The freezer on top has lots of different flavors of popsicles.

I leave the lounge and make my way down the hall again. It's clear to me now that the floor is a big circle. As I walk, I notice that the patient rooms are on my right side, and there are nurses' stations and conference rooms on my left. I notice one door marked "Social Worker." Dr. Tyrell told me that the social worker will be my new best friend. I make a note to meet with her on Monday. There doesn't seem to be anyone there today.

There are several nurses moving in and out of patient rooms. All of a sudden, I hear a clattering behind me—a little boy of about five is barreling toward me on a Big Wheel tricycle.

"Get out of the waaaayyyyyy!" he bellows, as he blows by me. He makes a sharp right turn into a room. I peek in as I pass by. He hops up onto the bed and grabs a game controller. A woman who I'm guessing is his mom sits on the couch, peering at a laptop.

We briefly make eye contact as I walk by.

I complete about three-quarters of the loop, and I'm on my way back to Angie's room. On my right is a playroom—two teenagers with name badges are in there, coloring with two little girls. The teens must be volunteers. The little girls are obviously patients. Neither of them have any hair, and they both have IV poles within easy reach.

The room is on the outside wall of the hospital and a huge window lets in a ton of sunlight. Two walls are lined with cubbies that hold games, toys, and puzzles. It's very organized. In the corner stands a TV with an

Xbox, and a couple of gaming chairs. It seems like the perfect place for a kiddo to go to when they are sick of their room.

One of the pumps on a pole starts beeping, and a volunteer reaches up to turn it off. I see her push a button on the wall and talk into it—I can't hear anything through the glass walls and door. Just a few seconds later a nurse comes down the hall and enters the playroom to check out the situation.

Angie's room is just a few doors down from the playroom. I start walking again and almost run into a dad chasing after a little girl. She can't be older than two and she's running like a tiger is chasing her. Her dad follows behind her, pushing her IV pole and doing his best to keep up with her. She's laughing and screeching with joy.

Overall the floor seems bright and cheery. There's a lot of natural light, and they seem to offer everything that a family might need for a long stay. And all of the kids still want to run, ride bikes, and play games, just like any other kid in the world.

But almost every child I see is dragging an IV pole behind them. I've always heard that little kids are resilient—they can adapt to almost anything. So far, the children on this floor are proving that to be true.

Chapter Seven

Three hours after Angie is wheeled through the double doors, they wheel her back into her room. I'm stretched out on the couch reading *The Hate U Give* when the bed rolls through the door, followed by Mr. and Mrs. Gutiérrez.

I stand up and look at Angie. She's still knocked out. Her eyes are closed and she doesn't seem to hear the conversation that her parents are having. Just like the doctor had explained, a catheter is hanging out of her neck. There are three lines that are visible, protruding from a bandage that covers the incision where the catheter is inserted. Each line is sealed with a cap.

A smiling nurse enters the room, carrying an IV bag.

"Hi everybody! Looks like we have quite the party

happening in here."

She hangs the bag on the IV pole and looks at Angie, who's just starting to open her eyes.

"Hey, sleepyhead, wanna start waking up?"

"I guess…" Angie's speech is slurred, but her eyes are opening a bit wider.

"Would you like some apple juice? And maybe some goldfish?"

Angie's eyes open wider. "Sure," she says.

The nurse leaves the room, and Angie's parents and I are left alone standing around the bed, looking at Angie. An IV line is in the back of the right hand, and that catheter looks like a three-headed snake that's exploding from her neck.

I look at her parents' faces. I always thought they were so cute and young looking, but now they look like they've aged twenty years since yesterday. I suppose stress can do that.

I put my arm around Mrs. Gutiérrez' shoulders and say to her, "You should go home and rest for a while. I'll be here with Angie."

"I don't know…." She looks at her husband, to see what he's thinking.

"I think if Cassidy is willing to help, we should let her," he says. "Angie won't be alone." Mr. G. is a smart man.

"Okay. I can make some food to bring to the hospital, too. She'll get tired of the hospital food very soon."

Angie's mom tries to feed us constantly, even though she works full time. And that reminds me of something I want to talk to her about.

"I know that you'll need to keep working. I'm happy to spend as much time here as I can. I'll come straight from school every day."

"Oh, honey, you don't have to do that..." Mrs. Gutiérrez begins—but then her hubby cuts her off. He knows a good thing when he sees one!

"We'll both need to work at least part time. Let's discuss this more once we have a diagnosis and a treatment plan. But, this will definitely be a team effort. And we really appreciate your offer, Cassidy."

Angie's dad puts his arms around me and actually gives me a hug! He has never done that before in all the years we've known each other. I hug him back, tightly.

They spend a few minutes chatting with Angie and telling her they'll be back later. They give her smooches and leave.

"Do you feel like watching TV?" I ask her.

"Nah, it's okay. I'm still a little sleepy."

I decide that this sounds like the perfect time to check my Facebook and Insta. I grab my laptop from my backpack and connect to the hospital Wi-Fi.

"Hey!" I exclaim, as a thought hits me. "Can I create a Facebook page for you, so we can update people about what's going on with you? We can have a hashtag, too, like *#AwesomeAngie*. What do you think?"

Before she has a chance to answer, I start searching Facebook for the words "leukemia" and "cancer." There are plenty of pages that support kids and adults. I see hashtags for *#TeamBennett* and *#Love4Lainey*.

"How about *#AngieStrong*? All of these are about fighting."

Angie pushes the button on her remote control to raise the head of the bed, so she has a better view of what I'm working on. I'm totally focused on building this new page. Or, maybe it should be a group, instead of a page.

"I don't know if I want all this attention, Cass."

I stop pounding the keyboard and look at her. Well, crap. I don't want to do anything that will upset her. She has enough on her plate.

"I'm sorry, Ange, I don't want to do anything that bothers you. But you have a ton of friends, and they'll want to know how you're doing, and how they can help."

Just then, my brain-lightbulb glows really bright.

"We could make a closed group, so we can control who reads about you. Would you be okay with that? I'll keep the riff-raff out, I promise."

She smiles at me. "Sure, that's okay. You keep everybody posted for me. So I don't have to."

"You got it! You'll have the best cancer group on Facebook."

"Oh, that's just wonderful!" She throws the tissue box at me. I don't duck in time.

There are two sharp knocks on the door, and then it opens. I wonder why people bother knocking, if they're just going to walk in the room anyway.

Instead of another nurse or doctor coming through the door, a large machine is rolling in. It's about three and a half feet tall, with lots of knobs and buttons. Like the IV pole next to Angie's bed, there are bags hanging from it. But these bags aren't full—they're empty.

"Well, hi there, ladies!" Two women come into view behind the machine. Both wear the blue scrubs that almost everyone else in the hospital seems to wear. One woman is very tall—she must be over six-feet. Her brunette hair is piled on top of her head in a messy bun, and a pencil sticks out of it.

The other woman is Black, and her hair is cropped close to her scalp. She's the one who originally said hello to us.

"We're with Carter Bloodcare, and we'll be in charge of your apheresis today. My name is Keisha and this is Sandy."

The brunette woman waves in our direction—she doesn't seem very talkative.

"So, here's how this is gonna work," says Keisha, as she rolls the machine close to Angie's bed. "We're going to connect the tubes at the end of your catheter to this machine. It's going to slowly remove some of the blood from your body. Then the machine will spin it around really fast, and remove only the white cells. Then the rest of the blood will go back into your body. Isn't that the coolest thing?"

Angie gives me a little bit of side-eye at the comment about the "coolest thing." I think we could both think of many things cooler than all of the blood being sucked out of your body, and then put back in.

"How long will it take?" asks Angie.

"Oh, about three hours. We don't want to take out the blood too fast. That wouldn't be good. There are two of us here, because a technician always needs to monitor the machine. So if one of us needs a potty break, the other will be here to make sure nothing goes wrong. Okay?"

Angie nods, but she looks nervous. She has completely woken from the earlier anesthesia and scoots up to a sitting position in bed.

"Is it going to hurt?"

"Oh no, honey, not at all," Keisha tells her. "But you'll be hooked up to this machine for about three hours. If you need to use the restroom, you should do that now."

During the next three hours we watch four episodes of *The Office*, and then we switch to *Friends*. I decide to do a little exploring and find the hospital cafeteria on the lower level. They have a lovely selection of salads, soup, and fresh fruit, but oh-my-god the sweet potato fries are to die for! I bring an order back to Angie's room, along with a bottled Frappuccino.

I finish creating the new Facebook group and invite just a few people to it. The pinned post at the top gives a brief explanation of what is going on. I grab the best photo I can find of the two of us as the cover image—it's from a track meet, of course. Angie has her arm around my neck and she's grinning from ear-to-ear. She just won (again) and can't hide how happy she is.

"Okay, it looks like we're all done!" Keisha is looking at the bag hanging above the apheresis machine. It's about three quarters full of what looks like a thick, orange liquid.

I stand up and walk over to get a closer look.

"What is that?" I ask.

"These are Angie's white blood cells; the ones that are taking up too much room inside her body."

"Wow—what are you going to do with them?"

"We'll dispose of them properly. We won't just pour them down the drain," she says, laughing.

Keisha hands a disposable behind-the-ear mask to me, Angie, and Sandy, then puts one over her own mouth and nose. The rest of us do the same.

"We can't let any of our germs get into this line while it's disconnected," she explains. "All righty, let's disconnect you, sweetheart."

In just a couple of minutes Angie's catheter is disconnected from the machine. Angie thanks Keisha for her help. She's always so polite—even in the freaking hospital!

"You're welcome, darlin'. If you need apheresis again, I might see you. Have a good evening!"

Sandy holds the door open for Keisha and the big machine she's pushing in front of her. As they clear the doorway, Mrs. Gutiérrez walks in.

"Hi Mama," Angie greets her.

"How do you feel?"

"I'm fine. Cassidy brought me sweet potato fries."

"Ah, that's nice." Mrs. Gutiérrez looks at me, a sad smile on her face. "You're a wonderful friend, Cassidy. More like a sister."

She had never said anything like that to me before—I can feel my eyes welling up, but I don't want to cry in front of either one of them.

"Oh, you know, Mrs. Gutiérrez, I'd do anything for Angie. She'd do the same for me."

"I know, honey, I know. Listen, Cassidy, you should go home. I'm here now, and I'm going to stay for a while. You go get ready for school tomorrow."

"Oh, okay."

"I'm going to call the school first thing tomorrow morning and tell them what's happening. Can you check in with Angie's teachers and see if they have homework for her?"

"Sure, I can do that. I'll be back here right after school, too," I tell her. Then I remember what Dr. Tyrell at Urgent Care had said. "Tomorrow, you should also check in with the social worker. I don't think they're here today, but the doctor at Urgent Care said it's important to talk to them."

"Ah, okay, that's good to know. I'll make sure that I do that tomorrow. You go home and get some rest. Get ready for school tomorrow." She puts her arms around me and hugs me tight.

I gather up my laptop and backpack and say good-bye to Angie and her mom. Leaving is weird. I kind of want to go, and I kind of don't. I feel guilty, like I'm letting Angie and her mom down by going home.

At the door I turn and look back at them. They're looking at the in-room menu, thinking about getting some dinner. Angie looks up at me. Damn, she looks pretty pathetic with those tubes hanging out of her neck. She's so pale, too. It's hard to believe that she just won a track competition the day before.

"What?" she asks me.

"Nothing. I'll see you tomorrow."

"Okay. You look worried. Don't worry. It's all good." She smiles at me.

"Yeah, I know it is." I open the door and leave for the evening.

Chapter Eight

One Year Earlier

"Remember, don't touch your face after you pick those peppers!" Angie's mom reminded us every single time we came over to pick jalapeños.

She had about a dozen plants in her backyard that were bursting with the super-spicy peppers. We needed to pick them now, at their peak, and then Mrs. Gutiérrez would preserve them in several different ways. My favorite was the pickled jalapeños that we would add to nachos and fajitas—sometimes, Angie and I would eat them straight out of the jar as a midnight snack.

We each had a large woven basket that we dropped the peppers into. They were all about three or four inches long and most were bright green, but there were also some that had started turning red. Angie said those probably should have been picked a little sooner, but would still be good. They might be a tad less spicy, but they would still be tasty.

It was a gorgeous day in early October. We both wore floppy sun hats to keep our faces from getting burned. Honestly, I didn't think I'd ever seen Angie with a sunburn. Her skin just became more golden, the longer she was in the sun. I was the pasty white girl, who burned to a crisp if I didn't slather on the SPF 30.

I looked past the pepper garden, to the small hill in the corner of the backyard. The pumpkin patch was overflowing with pumpkins of all sizes. Angie and I would soon choose our favorites that we could carve into Jack O'Lanterns, then the rest would go to the neighborhood kids. I loved being in this garden. There was so much life—even the water in the little pond sounded bubbly and happy. There were about seven goldfish that Angie and I had named years ago. My favorite was Pinky Pie, but she looked an awful lot like Mrs. Potts these days. I really couldn't tell them apart. They were both about three inches long and bright orange.

When our baskets were full and not a pepper remained on the plants, we brought them into the kitchen and dumped them in the sink. Mrs. Gutiérrez gave them a quick rinse and then laid them out to dry on a layer of kitchen towels.

On the stove, a pot full of pickling brine was simmering. The vinegary, sugary goodness smelled like heaven. I couldn't wait to pour it over the peppers.

"Okay, girls, let's get to slicing!" Angie's mom handed both of us a pair of latex gloves. While she had warned us about touching our faces while we were picking the peppers, it was way more serious when we were slicing them.

The first time we helped with the pepper harvest I didn't take the offer of gloves seriously. We were both twelve, and I thought I knew better. A little pepper couldn't hurt me—what was she talking about? I learned my lesson quickly, and as Angie helped flush my eyes with water I vowed to never slice a spicy pepper without gloves again.

The peppers that were lying on the kitchen towels to dry would be loaded into a plastic bag and stored in the freezer to be used throughout the year.

That morning, Mrs. Gutiérrez had picked several pounds of her tomatillos. It amazed me, how many of them grew on one plant. I think she ended up with about five pounds—that was plenty for a huge bowl of salsa verde and some left over to store in the freezer for later.

She peeled the papery husks off of the green fruit that looked just like an unripe regular tomato. But for some reason the salsa she made with these babies was so much tastier than the red salsa. At least, that was my opinion. Once they were peeled, Mrs. Gutiérrez cut them in half and put them under the broiler in the oven until the skins turned black. Then she threw them in the blender along with onion, garlic, plenty of jalapeños, lime juice, cilantro, and a little salt.

It was the absolute best salsa in the world—last year, she'd even entered it in the State Fair of Texas and won a blue ribbon. When I asked what it was about the recipe that made it so delicious, she explained, "It's not the recipe, Cassidy. It's the technique and the ingredients. Many traditionalists boil the tomatillos in a big pot of water to make them soft, but sticking them under the broiler gives them so much more flavor. Sometimes I'll roast the garlic with them, but I didn't do that today. And when almost all of the ingredients come from my garden, you won't find a fresher batch of salsa verde."

That night Angie and I stayed up late watching movies. I was sunburned, she wasn't, and we were both eating more chips and salsa than we should have.

It was perfect.

Chapter Nine

I'm standing at my locker the next morning getting ready for my first class when Miranda suddenly appears next to me. Miranda, with her cute, dark pixie cut that no one but she can pull off. Every other girl in our school has long hair flowing past their shoulders, but not Miranda. That hairstyle marks her as a rebel.

She and I have been mortal enemies since eighth grade, when she caught me kissing her brother. It had been at Miranda's thirteenth birthday party. Her brother, Jeff, is a year older than us. He had asked me if I had ever kissed a boy, and I told him no. So he kissed me. I didn't think it was a big deal, and it wasn't anything to write home about. His lips were really chapped.

But Miranda was pissed. And then we weren't

friends anymore.

So as she walks up to me on an already crappy Monday morning with her dark hair framing her pretty face, I'm already preparing myself for some kind of fight.

"I heard about Angie being in the hospital," is how she greets me.

This is a surprise. I certainly hadn't told Miranda about Angie's cancer, and I don't think Angie had.

"You did? How?"

"From the Facebook group. Stacie invited me."

Oh, that's right. I invited a few of Angie's and my friends and gave them the ability to invite more people.

"I want to help. What does she need?"

This is an even bigger surprise.

"Um, I'm not sure. This whole thing is still pretty new. I'm not sure what she needs."

"How about a GoFundMe? I'm sure this is going to be expensive. I'll set up a GoFundMe. If there's anything else she needs, let me know."

She turns on her Steve Madden heels and walks away.

Huh—maybe she isn't all that bad. Still kind of annoying but not all bad.

I grab my backpack from my locker and head to my first class. The halls are jam-packed—they always are. There are way too many kids at my high school so getting to class always feels like being a salmon swimming upstream.

As I make my way through the throng, I'm thinking about Miranda's offer and her initial question.

"What does Angie need?"

I need to think about that. Most people are probably going to come to me with that question, and right now, I don't know the answer. I try to put myself in her shoes. What will she do all day? There's a TV in her room, and she has her laptop, but you can only watch so much Netflix, Hulu, and Prime.

I know that getting chemo treatments sucks. Well, I don't really know how much it sucks, of course. But I'm sure it does.

What is she going to feel like doing while she's cooped up in the hospital? I have no idea.

I actually make it to first period Language Arts a few minutes early. I walk into the classroom, and like every morning, a feeling of peace washes over me. It's probably similar to what walking into a church is like for a lot of people. For me, it's my Language Arts class taught by Ms. Malone.

I've been lucky enough to have her as a teacher for the past three years. We began our bookish relationship in eighth grade, when she introduced me to Stephen King. I don't know how many nights I stayed up late, scaring myself to death. I loved every minute of it.

Then when I moved over to the high school, so did she! At first, I was sure that she was following me— how could she stand to be apart from her most favorite student ever? But then I found out that there had been an opening that included a raise for her. It doesn't matter—I still make sure that I'm able to work every single class she teaches into my schedule.

Ms. Malone is at her desk, thumbing through our latest reading assignment. Her dark hair is cut in a cute bob that comes just to her chin. Her eyes are framed by large red glasses.

"Hi Ms. Malone. Do you have a minute?"

"Oh, hi, Cassidy. Of course, what's up?" She stands and comes around to the front of her desk to talk to me.

"Do you know what's going on with Angie?"

"You mean that she's in the hospital?" When I nod, she continues. "Yes, we all received an e-mail this morning telling us about her. I'm so sorry, honey. I know that you're close."

I feel a little lump in my throat and I need to cough a little before I can speak.

"I said that I would bring her homework to her. Do you have anything?"

"Well, not really. I think for now, she should concentrate on getting healthy. School will be here when she's ready."

"Oh. Okay." How would I help now? I promised that I would collect Angie's assignments from her teachers, and now there are no assignments.

Ms. Malone is looking at me, a small smile on her face.

"You're not sure how to help her, right?"

I'm not all that surprised that she knows what's bugging me. She's always very insightful—she seems to just get what's going on with me. That's why she's my favorite teacher.

"Yeah, I guess that's true. I thought this was the one thing that I could do for her. I don't really know what else there is."

"Oh, Cassidy, that's not true. You're her best friend. When the time comes, you'll know exactly what she needs."

I sigh. "I suppose."

"This is still very new. It will take time to figure out a plan for treatment, and how everyone will be able to help. You don't have to figure everything out right now. I'll help you and Angie any way that I can. Okay?"

"Okay."

The door to the classroom opens and students begin pouring in, dumping their backpacks onto desks. I make it over to my desk and sit down.

Language Arts moves on as if it's any other day. We start reading a modern telling of *Taming of the Shrew*. Normally, I love this kind of story. Today, I can barely concentrate, and I can't understand how anyone else in the class is able to. We're all Angie's friends—aren't they wondering what the hell is happening at the hospital, like I am?

I don't know how I'm going to get through this day, if I can't even concentrate in my favorite class. How the hell would I handle Geometry?

Lunchtime finally rolls around. I'm standing in the food line waiting patiently for my chicken nuggets. School is the only place I can eat deep-fried, gluten-filled goodness. At home, Mom makes sure that I eat healthy. I don't really mind—she's an excellent cook. But at school I make sure to take advantage of the delicious unhealthiness.

Suddenly, I feel someone grab me from behind and squeeze me in a tight bear hug. It can only be one person. I stomp on the humongous foot that is next to mine, and I'm free.

"Ow!" yells Sam. "Was that necessary?"

I turn to face him.

"Yes, it was, butthead."

I have to crane my neck back to look up at him, since he's at least eight inches taller than me. Tall and wiry, he's the fastest boy on the track team. His curly brown hair is practically sticking straight up from his head. Today he's wearing jeans and an ancient Styx concert T-shirt—the kind with three-quarter length sleeves, that looks like a baseball jersey. I notice the date on the shirt.

"1981, huh? Is that your dad's shirt?"

"No, my mom's. She used to be cool and go to lots of concerts. She has a ton of these."

"Hey, your mom's still cool! I love her. And I especially love the bread that she bakes."

Sam's mom has a small baking business that she runs out of her home kitchen. Her specialty is sourdough bread. I could eat that stuff all day long. Carbs? Who cares! Even my health conscious mom approves of sourdough baked goodies—she said that people who have a hard time tolerating gluten don't have as much trouble with breads that aren't baked with commercial yeast. Works for me! Her bread definitely tastes better than anything you can buy at the store.

I place my tray where the lunch lady can reach it.

"Hey, Mrs. Browne! How are things today?" Mrs. Browne's youngest son is Devon, who is in my American History class. We go way back.

"Good, Cassidy! We have fish tacos today. How's that sound?"

"Sounds yummy! Pile a couple on here!"

Sam ends up with five fish tacos, plus chips and salsa. I'm happy with the two tacos on my plate. We make our way to our usual table and sit down. Our butts barely have time to hit the folding benches before Miranda sits beside me.

I look at her in surprise, holding one of my tacos in front of my mouth.

"What?" I ask her.

"I've been working on the GoFundMe. I wanted to show you." She places an iPad on the table in front of me.

This is too weird. This girl hasn't spoken two words to me in years, and now she willingly comes up to me twice in one day. And she isn't being mean.

"Miranda, what's going on? Why are you being nice?" I know that sounds bitchy—I don't care. It's the truth.

She looks down at the tablet while she speaks to me.

"I might have some experience with cancer. I know how much it sucks. For a lot of different reasons."

"What kind of experience?" I ask.

"I don't like to talk about it. But it might be important to you and Angie."

"Okay…" I have no idea what she's talking about.

"When I was seven, my three-year-old brother was diagnosed with leukemia."

This isn't making any sense. Miranda has an older brother—the one I kissed. But she doesn't have a younger brother. I would have known about that.

"What are you talking about?" I ask her. "Your brother is older than you—it's Jeff!"

I know that I'm coming across as pretty condescending, and I kinda feel bad about it. But, really, she's acting like an idiot!

For some reason, Miranda is looking at me as if I'm the idiot. She rolls her eyes so high that for a second I'm only looking at the whites of her eyes.

"I will speak slowly, so you understand," she tells me. "When I was seven, I had a three-year-old brother. He had leukemia. He died. I don't like to talk about it. But I'll talk to you, because I think it might help Angie."

Ohhhhhhh. Geez, I feel dumb.

"Miranda, I'm so sorry." My voice is barely louder than a whisper. "We've known each other for a long time, and I never heard about this. That's why I acted so stupid. I'm really sorry."

Her face relaxes, and she doesn't look quite as annoyed with me as she had been. "No, I get it. My family never talks about him, or what he went through. We kind of buried everything when he died."

She's quiet for a moment. The expression on her face is so sad. She must have loved her little brother very much.

"I don't think that was the right thing for us to do. But at the time, I couldn't do anything about it. I was so little."

I gaze at Miranda as she speaks. I don't know what to say. Does she want to talk about her brother, or not? I'm really afraid of saying or doing the wrong thing.

Maybe if I just say, "I'm sorry," it will help.

I open my mouth to speak, but no words come out; just a weird sound from deep in my throat. It sounds like a cross between a squeak and a belch. I slap my hand over my mouth, in an attempt to keep any other weird sounds from escaping.

Miranda's fist slams the top of the table. My tray jumps and my water bottle almost falls over. I have no idea what I did to make her so mad! I haven't even said anything!

"God damn it!" the words explode from her mouth. "This is what I'm talking about. I can tell, Cassidy, I can see it all over your face. You're afraid to talk about him. You don't want to say the wrong thing, because you might upset me."

She's right. I just nod; I don't utter a sound.

"That's the problem! We need to talk about it. We

need to remember my brother and not pretend that he was never born. And we need to talk about fucking cancer, because it's real. And families who are going through it shouldn't feel like they're going through it alone. *That*'s why we need to help Angie and her family."

I am stunned. I never knew that Miranda feels this passionately about...anything. And I feel horrible. I wish I had known about everything Miranda and her family went through and that I had been there to help her. Sure, I would have been a seven-year-old kid also, but I might have been able to do something for her.

I place my hand over her clenched fist.

"You're right," I tell her. "I want to hear about your brother. I want to look at pictures of him. I want to know what I should do for Angie and her family."

Chapter Ten

Miranda is an organizational machine. She wants to take over the Facebook page, so I let her. I'm sure to let her know that Angie doesn't want a ton of attention on Facebook; it should only be for friends and family.

"I can do that," she assures me. Her fingers fly across the keyboard of her laptop as she talks to me. "I get that there's kind of a fine line. I'll definitely make sure that the trolls stay away."

We're hanging out in Ms. Malone's classroom after school, while she's grading papers. I love being in that room after school. It's so quiet and peaceful; the afternoon sun is shining in the windows, making this feel so warm and cozy.

Miranda is quickly filling a spiral notebook with ideas that are popping into her head. She arbitrarily says something like, "I bet Angie will be able to get all kinds of scholarships when she's healthy again. There's a ton of stuff here for cancer survivors."

"That's really cool, but she doesn't need to worry about that for a while. Let's get her healthy first." I need to keep reeling her back in. She's like a dog being constantly distracted by a new squirrel.

"What do we have so far?" I ask.

She turns the laptop a smidge so I can see the screen better.

"So far I have the Facebook group. It's private, so I need to approve members. That'll help keep out the randos. I also have a CaringBridge site. Sometimes grandparents aren't on Facebook, so they can get updates here instead. I also started a GoFundMe."

That one surprised me a bit. "Really? Do you think that's necessary? I mean, we don't know if they need money."

"Cassidy," Miranda gives me some serious side-eye as she addresses me. "Of course, they're going to need money. Until my brother got sick, both of my parents were working. They had good jobs. We lived in a nice house. Christmas and birthdays were great. And then when my brother was diagnosed, my mom had to quit her job. Caring for someone with cancer is full-time."

"Even when he was in the hospital?" I asked. I would think that the doctors and nurses would take care of him.

"Oh, yeah, especially when he was in the hospital. Every patient needs an advocate."

"What do you mean?" I ask. "Like someone to talk to the doctors?"

"Yeah, and other things." Miranda is still focused on the GoFundMe page. "Trust me, Angie's parents are gonna need all the help they can get. And that includes help with money."

I'm beginning to realize how much more Miranda understands about this than I do.

"I trust you," I tell her.

"So, I also have a Meal Train schedule set up. They are *not* going to have time to cook, and who wants fast-food every day?"

Ms. Malone glances up from the papers she's grading. Miranda doesn't notice it because she's so engrossed in all of the different tabs that are open on her computer. But I do. Ms. Malone smiles at me. She approves of this plan, I can tell.

But I'm starting to think about Angie—a lot. I miss her. I feel that I need to be in the hospital with her.

"Miranda," I say. "Let's stop for tonight. I need to go to the hospital."

"No, no, wait! This is the last thing we need to do. We need to set up a visitation calendar. The most important thing for Angie is for her friends to visit her."

"Are you sure? Don't you think she'll need as much peace and quiet as she can get?"

"Nope! She's gonna be bored stiff. She'll definitely want company."

This girl is on fire! She's creating a spreadsheet and entering all the names of Angie's friends in the first column. Every member of the track team is listed, and so is our old Girl Scout troop. We haven't been in Scouts for years, but Miranda remembers them all.

The second column is for the date they would visit Angie, the third is for the time of day, and the fourth is for the duration of that visit. In the last column, Angie's friends are supposed to make a note of what they would bring her. A snack, a book, or some other small gift.

"The main point of this is to make sure that people are visiting her. And, that they don't just come in the beginning, but then stop as time goes on," Miranda explained. "That happened to us. Everyone was all concerned and helpful during the first couple of months, and then they just kinda forgot about us. I know that people are busy, but it really sucked."

She had created the spreadsheet using Google Sheets, so anyone could update it with their own schedules. Ms. Malone suggests that we ask the principal if an announcement could be made during the scheduled morning message.

"Yes!" Miranda interjects, "and we'll need to make sure that they mention it every day, otherwise people will forget."

"I can make sure that will happen," Ms. Malone says as she stands up behind her desk. "But now, my darlings, it's late. I need to get home, and so do you.'"

Miranda quickly saves her documents, exits out of the various tabs, and closes her laptop.

Ms. Malone is right—the warm afternoon sunlight that had been streaming through the windows just a few moments ago is practically gone. It's almost dark outside.

I sling my backpack over my shoulder.

"Miranda, do you want to come to the hospital with me?" I ask.

"No, not tonight. I'm going home to do some homework and finish working on this stuff for Angie."

Then, she smiles at me. It's the smile I remember from sixth grade when we did everything together. I feel all melty inside.

"Okay, great," I reply.

She shrugs her backpack on over both shoulders—the right way, so she isn't carrying too much weight on one side of her back.

"I'll come with you another night this week. Promise."

Chapter Eleven

It's close to eight when I finally make it to the hospital. I grab some Whataburger fries on the way down. They're Angie's favorites. There are a few In-and-Out stores in our area, but I never understood why people think they're so great. Whataburger is the only burger I'll ever eat.

I quickly get my badge from the security desk—I'm in their system now, so it doesn't take long. There's a different feeling in the hospital at night. It's calmer and quieter than it is during the day. When the sun is shining through the windows and the skylights, and nurses and doctors are bustling from one floor to the next, there's a busy energy in the air.

Now it's dark except for the electric lights. Hardly anyone is on the first floor as I make my way to the elevators. No one joins me in the car, and no one is waiting in the reception area on the sixth floor.

I walk through the quiet, dimly-lit hallways until I get to Angie's room. But I stop in front of the door, because something feels off. I can't put my finger on it; and then I realize that the window no longer depicts the Beauty and the Beast characters. A fantastic tree has been painted on the window, filled with colorful birds and flowers. Among the branches I can see a small figure that looks just like Angie. It's incredible.

I open the door and enter the room.

"Hey, hey, I have French fries!" I announce.

She's alone, snoozing in her bed. I'm kind of surprised to see that she's wearing the Pooh-Bear pajamas she bought the last time the two of us went to Target. I guess I assumed that when you're in the hospital, you need to wear the flimsy gown they give everyone.

The bright overhead lights are turned off, but the room is illuminated by a soft, green glow. On the ceiling a border of painted fish are swimming in a green ocean. The painting encircles the entire room. The TV is on, but the volume is turned all the way down. At first I think that Angie is asleep, but then she turns her head toward me and opens her eyes.

"Oh, god, are those Whataburger fries?" Angie's eyes grow huge and she sits up in bed, reaching for one of the bags I'm carrying. She rips it open lengthwise, down the side, and digs in. A true French fry connoisseur, she doesn't use ketchup. I, on the other hand, can't have a bit of fry in my mouth unless it's slathered in ketchup.

"What happened at school today?" Angie asks, in between bites. She still has the catheter hanging out of her neck. They must not be finished with apheresis.

"Well, nobody has any schoolwork for you to do yet. They told me not to worry about it. Did the doctors tell you anything more today?"

"Yeah, they figured out what I have. It's ALL—stands for Acute Lymphoblastic Leukemia. They said that chemo should cure it, but I'll need to stay in the hospital for a month. It's called 'induction.'"

"A month! Holy crap!" I sputter these words around a mouthful of fries.

"I know. It sucks. My mom is going to take a month off from work, and then we'll see what we need to do after that."

"God, a month seems like forever." I look around the bare, sterile hospital room, and an idea starts to form in my head. "We'll decorate your room for Halloween. "

"You better! We still need to decide on costumes."

"Oh, I've been thinking about that! What about if you're Bob Ross, and I could be your painting? Or, I could be Mr. Rogers and you could be a puppet!"

Angie grins and reaches for another fry. "Would you be Sexy Mr. Rogers? I saw a picture of that floating around on Facebook. "

I pull a face and say, "Hell, no, I don't think I want to do that! Oh, wait, I know!" I have a great idea—I'm waving my French fry in Angie's face when I say, "Let's be Baby Sharks!"

She starts laughing and swats my hand that's holding the perfectly fried potatoes.

"Okay, okay if it makes you happy! But I want to be Mommy Shark. She's the coolest."

"Hey, look what I got today." She pulls the top of her PJ top down and exposes an area on the upper-right side of her chest. There's a bump, with a tube sticking out of it. They're both covered with a sticky, plastic tape.

I must be staring at it with a very confused expression on my face, because Angie feels the need to explain.

"It's my port!"

A port. Okay....

"Ange, I'm sorry, I need more."

"They use it instead of an IV. I'm pretty much connected to this pole all the time, but it's better than having a needle stuck in my arm."

I move a little closer to her, to get a better look. I can't see a needle—but it doesn't look very comfortable.

"It doesn't hurt?"

"Eh, it's a little annoying, but it doesn't hurt."

I start to get a little thirsty, after ingesting all of this salty, potato-y goodness and chatting about Angie's new port.

"I wish I had a milkshake or something to dip these in," I tell Angie.

"Oh, I can help with that!" She swings her legs over the bed and shoves her feet in her flip flops. She unplugs her IV pole from the power outlet and swings the cord over the top of the whole contraption. "Let's go get some ice cream!"

I'm a little bit shocked. I think she probably needs to stay in her bed and not go anywhere. Except, maybe, to the bathroom.

She grabs her pole and pushes it in front of her as she makes her way out of the room. Angie maneuvers that thing as if it's a part of her. It's so strange to me— the last time I saw her, she didn't have this extra appendage. Now, it's like she's never been without it.

We pass by the tall desk where the nurses are chatting and checking on patient files. There's a lot of beeping going on at that desk, but no one seems too worried about all the noise.

A head full of bright red curls suddenly pops up.

"Hey ladies, is everything all right?

"Hi Sheila," says Angie. "We're going to get some ice cream."

"Sounds good! I'll be in your room in about 15 minutes for your 9:00 meds, okay?"

"Okay, that works." Angie pushes her pole forward and leads us down the hall.

There's a ton of ice cream in the freezer. It's in a small, doorless room labeled "Nutrition." But it's really just a small kitchen, minus a stove. Two microwave ovens sit on the counter-top, and there are two refrigerators. Both contain instructions about how the patients' food need to be stored.

Place food in a large Ziploc bag, labeled with the patient's name. Make sure you label it with the current date. All food over 48 hours old will be discarded.

That seems a little over-the-top, but I suppose they know what they're doing.

Angie is digging through the freezer, apparently looking for something.

"Ah, here we go! I think I found the last four vanilla cups. Let's go finish those fries!"

We settle back into her room, dipping our Whataburger fries into semi-melted vanilla ice cream. It's pretty darn tasty.

I'm deep into an ice cream coated fry when I hear Angie clear her throat.

"So," another throat clear. "There's something they told me that I didn't really understand."

"Oh yeah? What's that?" The ice cream is starting to seriously melt—it's dripping down my fingers.

"Well, today one of the doctors told me that my leukemia is 'very high risk.' I know that it's because I'm over thirteen and my white count was so high, but I don't really know what that means."

"Did you or your mom ask them what it means?"

"No, I didn't." She sounds a little ashamed, as if she should have known better. I don't think that was something she should be worrying about.

"Look," I begin, "they're throwing so much information at you. You can't be expected to remember and understand absolutely everything they tell you, especially not the first time."

"Yeah, I guess that's true. My mom seemed pretty overwhelmed with all of the information, also. She just sat there the whole time the doctor was talking, nodding."

"Were either of you taking notes, or anything?"

Angie lets out a big sigh.

"No, we didn't think about that until later. That was pretty stupid."

"No, it's not," I reassure her. "You have so much to think about right now."

I'm thinking that there has to be a way to get that information—even at 9:00 at night.

"I'll be right back," I say, as I stand and walk toward the door. "I have an idea."

I'm thinking about what Miranda said, about every patient needing an advocate. It isn't surprising to me that Angie and her mom have just been so flustered and haven't been able to absorb all of the information being thrown at them. But I can try and help them sort it out, and fill in the holes.

I approach the nurses' station—the nice woman with the red curls is there. She looks up and smiles at me.

"Hi honey," she greets me. "What can I do for you?"

"My friend, Angie, told me that the doctor explained some things to her and her mom about her leukemia and the treatment, but she doesn't remember everything they said. Is there somebody she can talk to now, to get some questions answered?"

"Of course! The nurse practitioner is here, and she can answer Angie's questions. I'll call her and have her come into the room."

On my way back to the room, I stop in the small kitchen and grab two chocolate ice cream cups, since we had already taken the last two vanilla. I still have fries that need dipping.

Angie was re-watching *Gilmore Girls*, so we spend the next 25 minutes engrossed in the love lives of Lorelei and Rory. Rory is starting her first semester at Yale, and is about to meet Logan for the first time. Ah, Logan! You either love him or hate him. Personally, I'm on Team Jess.

There's a soft knock on the door—it opens, and a young woman wearing pink PJ pants with unicorns jumping over rainbows splattered all over them walks in. Her blonde hair is pulled back in a tight ponytail. Her long-sleeved t-shirt is a very light blue that matches her eyes.

"Hi guys!"

Her smile is warm and bright. She glances at the TV and her smile widens.

"Oh, you're watching *Gilmore Girls*! I've watched the whole thing three times now. I was madly in love with Jess."

"Me, too!" Angie and I both shouted.

"Well, good! We have something in common. My name is Carrie, and I'm the nurse practitioner on duty tonight. I hear that you have some questions."

Angie explains that when the doctor talked to her and her mom earlier in the day, they didn't quite catch everything. Carrie drags one of the armchairs across the floor, until she's right next to Angie. I notice how she looks directly into Angie's eyes—some people might think it's a little creepy, but I think she does it because she really wants to hear what Angie has to say.

"There was so much information, and so many words that neither one of us understood."

Carrie is nodding her head, continuing to pay complete attention to Angie's words.

"I totally get that. Being diagnosed with a serious illness is very scary. You and your family are trying to wrap your heads around all of this. It's going to change everything, for all of you."

Wow. She just puts it all out on the table. No holding back.

"Let me ask you something," Carrie continues. "Is there anything specific that you'd like to ask me, or should I just go over the treatment plan? And, of course, you can interrupt me at any time. I'll do my best to let you know what you might be able to expect."

"There is…one thing that I'd like to understand." Angie is a bit hesitant when she says that.

"Sure, honey, what is it?"

"The doctor told me that my leukemia is 'very high risk.' Can you tell me what that means?"

"Of course," Carrie said. She's still very kind and caring, but a slight change comes over her face. She looks serious. It occurs to me that nurse practitioners in a children's hospital don't have an easy job. Cancer is scary—how can someone like Carrie give bad news to kids and their parents?

"I can talk to you about that," Carrie is saying. "Leukemia isn't classified like some other cancers. You might have heard the terms Stage One, Two, Three, and Four."

"Sure." Angie is nodding.

"Leukemia is a little different. The levels are Standard, High Risk, and Very High Risk. These are determined by various factors. Do you have any questions so far?"

"Well," Angie's voice is quiet. "I think they told me today that I'm Very High Risk."

"Yes, that's right."

"I don't know what that means."

"You want me to be completely honest with you, right Angie?"

"Yes, completely. I need to know what's happening and what might happen. Don't sugar-coat it."

Carrie smiles and squeezes Angie's hand.

"I'll always be upfront with you and let you know what to expect. But you need to understand that you have a lot of control over your treatment. You need to maintain a positive attitude. That's so important. It's amazing how your body can heal, if your mind is focused on healing, too. So, being in the Very High Risk category means that it will be more difficult to cure your cancer. The first reason is because you're over the age of 13. That's just normal. Everyone over 13 is bumped up a level. Next, it's because your white cell count was so high when you were diagnosed. It was

200,000 per microliter. You're an overachiever!"

We all giggle at that. But I don't think it's very funny.

I suddenly remember that I had promised to take notes. This is probably the type of thing I should be documenting word-for-word. I stealthily slide my laptop out of my backpack.

"You also have something called a Philadelphia-like chromosome. It's a genetic mutation that adds to the risk level of your leukemia."

She pauses and gazes at Angie's face. Angie is holding it together.

"Questions?"

"Will I be okay?"

"That is the most important question, isn't it? I wish I could look into a crystal ball and tell you that everything is going to turn out perfectly. I'm afraid that I can't do that."

"I know that. I don't want you to lie to me."

"You might be surprised to hear that there are parents who only want to hear good news. I understand that, but it isn't always realistic. But I can promise you that we will do everything we can to cure you. You're in one of the best hospitals in the country—and that's the truth. Should I tell you about the treatment plan?"

"Yes, but I do have a question first."

"Shoot!"

"What would happen if I didn't have any treatment at all. I'm not saying that's what I want to do—not at all. I'm just curious about that."

I'm actually really glad she asked this. My own morbid curiosity wants to know, also.

"You have an 'acute' type of leukemia. That word

'acute' says it all. It comes on hard and fast. A week ago you were fine—now you're in the freaking hospital with cancer. That's how acute leukemia works. If you don't move forward with treatment, then those cancerous white cells would keep multiplying. When you were diagnosed a few days ago they were at 200,000—in a week, they'd probably be close to one million. Those cells will clog every blood vessel in your body, so blood and oxygen can no longer reach any of your organs. Do you know what your organs do if blood can't get to them?"

Angie's voice is a whisper, "They stop working."

"Exactly. That's why it's absolutely vital to begin treatment as soon as possible."

Carrie pauses. "I know it's scary. But we've already started treating your leukemia. You have an excellent chance of kicking this thing in the butt."

"Okay. And I really do want you to be straight with me. I don't think it does me any good if I don't know the truth."

"You got it!" Carrie's mouth breaks into a wide grin. Her eyes are sparkling again. "Do you want to go over your treatment plan now?"

"Sure. Lay it on me."

"So, you're aware that we've already started our typical frontline treatment. That's the chemotherapy. Even though chemo sucks and makes you feel like crap, it works really well for leukemia. This cures leukemia in over 90% of patients."

"Will my hair fall out?"

Carrie reaches out her hand to brush Angie's bangs across her forehead.

"You do have gorgeous hair, sweetie. Yeah, I'm afraid it's going to fall out. But when you're all done with treatment, it will grow back and it will be just as beautiful."

"When will it start falling out?"

"Probably in a couple of weeks. Another side effect of the chemo is that you'll feel pretty crappy. Most people are very nauseous. Also, since the chemo is killing healthy blood cells as well as the cancer cells, your immune system won't be able to fight infections and disease like it normally would. You'll have to be extra careful about being around sick people—even a cold could turn into something serious. Then after 30 days of chemo, we will know if it worked, or if we need to move on to Plan B."

"Plan B?" Angie's voice is quiet.

"Plan B is actually really cool, and we've seen great results with it. It's called CAR T Cell Therapy."

"I remember hearing that word, but I don't remember what the doctor said about how it works."

"It is so cool!"

Carrie looks around the hospital room. She stands up and walks across the room to the small white board. The board has daily information on it, like who the nurse and doctor are for that day. With a paper towel, she wipes that board clean. She begins drawing what looks like little cartoon- type cells all over the board. Then on one side she labels the cells with a T, and on the other they are labeled with an L.

"All righty," she begins. "In our bodies, the T cells are our natural infection fighters. But in the case of leukemia, which is harder to fight, they need a little extra help. So we will take the T cells out of your body, using apheresis."

"Oh, yeah, they did that the other day. With the catheter in my neck."

"Exactly!" said Carrie. "It'll be just like that, except we'll be extracting T cells, instead of those crazy white cells. They spin around in the centrifuge machine, and the T cells are extracted. Then, they're sent to a lab in New Jersey where they are super-charged!"

With these words, Carrie outlines the T cells on the white board in sparks and flames.

"It takes about four weeks until they're ready. Then, we'll put them back into your body just like any other transfusion or medication."

"Into my port?" Angie asked.

"That's right! Then, those new super-charged cells will get to work. They're going to multiply and they'll attack and destroy the leukemia cells."

She's pretty aggressive with the marker, crossing out the cells that are marked with an L.

Angie is paying close attention. She chews her lower lip as she listens. I'm typing furiously, doing my best to capture all the information.

"That does sound really cool," she said. "And that will work, if the chemo doesn't?"

Carrie places the cap back on the dry erase marker she's holding.

"Honey, I can't promise that. It's different for everyone. We see amazing results with chemo, and also with CAR T. But there's no way that I can guarantee anything. We'll know after thirty days of treatment if the chemo is working, or if we need to move on to CAR T."

"Is there a Plan C, if Plan B doesn't work?"

Carrie sits back down on the chair next to Angie.

"Yes, there is!" she exclaims. "Plan C will be a bone marrow transplant. Have you heard of that?"

I focus on the notes I'm typing, but when I hear

the words, "bone marrow transplant" my fingers stop.

"Last year I signed up to be on that registry," I said. "There was a drive at school. A kid needed a bone marrow transplant. I think he had sickle cell disease. Does that sound right?"

"Absolutely! Bone marrow transplants cure lots of different diseases. Sickle cell is one of them. They just swabbed your mouth, right?"

I nod.

"Right—it was really easy." A thought occurs to me. "Is it that easy to actually donate the bone marrow?"

Carrie laughs. "Not quite that easy. The donor is given a general anesthetic, so they're completely asleep during the procedure. Then the marrow is extracted from their hip bone. They're a bit sore for a couple of days but that's it. And, of course, the bone marrow just regenerates. It's nothing like donating a solid organ."

"So," Angie pipes up, "is that how they would give me the new bone marrow? Would they put it in my bones?"

"That's a great question," says Carrie. "No, it actually is transfused using your port. Just like the blood transfusions, chemo, or those super-charged T cells. The bone marrow just knows where to go. It'll take a little while to engraft, but then it'll be producing brand new, healthy blood cells."

We are all quiet for a few moments, absorbing all of this information. I stare at my laptop screen, but I'm not really reading anything. I'm just thinking about Plan A, Plan B, and Plan C.

Instead of going home that night, I decide to sleep on the super-comfy pull-out couch in Angie's room. Yes, I'm being a tad sarcastic. But the nurse loads me up with sheets and hot blankets that come out of a warming cabinet. Oh, my goodness, I need to start warming my blankets at home. This is heaven!

The couch-bed thing is kinda weird. It isn't exactly a pull-out—there are cushions along the back that I need to lay down on top of the couch. That makes the whole lying-down area of the couch a bit bigger, because it becomes even with the arm rests. It's still on the small side. I can't imagine someone who's much bigger than me being comfortable. But I cover the mattress with the sheets and blankets and I'm sure I'll be fine.

I'm tucking in a blanket when the door opens, and a cart loaded with a TV is being pushed into the room.

A voice rings out from behind the cart.

"I hear we're having a sleepover tonight! I thought you ladies might like to use an Xbox."

"Sure," exclaims Angie. "Are there any racing games? I love car races."

As Angie browses the collection of games I help the woman, who we learn is with Child Life, plug the cart into a wall outlet. The cart itself is equipped with a power strip that we can use for the Xbox, and anything else that needs power, like my phone, which I realize is currently at eight percent. Whoops.

I turn on the TV and Xbox, and we all give a cheer when we realize that everything has power and seems to be properly connected. Woo hoo! We are the techie girls!

"Okay, ladies, looks like you're in business. Is there anything else I can get for you?"

We assure our Child Life friend that we are fine. She takes off, and we settle into several hours of Mario Kart.

STUCK

It's around midnight, and I'm starting to fade. Angie's still playing and doesn't look like she's ready to quit any time soon.

"I slept a lot today," she tells me. "And I'm on a roll! This is the most fun I've had in weeks!"

"Okay, that's fine," I reply. "But I'm done. Night, night." I snuggle myself under the blankets and rest my head on a very flat hospital pillow. I try to find one or two more, but apparently pillows are precious and hard to find. I'll make it work.

"Night, ni...oh, shit!" I glance at the TV—apparently, she barely avoided a serious crash.

Angie and her game might not let me get much sleep. I roll over onto my side and close my eyes.

Unfortunately, it isn't only Angie and her game that's keeping me up during the night. It seems like a nurse comes in the room every thirty minutes to check her IV, her blood pressure, and her temperature. Once they even woke Angie out of a sound sleep to make her swallow some pills.

I think it's around 5:00 a.m. when I finally doze off. The next thing I know, the sun is streaming through the windows and a group of people are standing around Angie's bed, talking about her.

They don't seem to notice me. I sit up and stay quiet, and after a few minutes they say good-bye to Angie and leave the room.

"Who were they?" I ask her.

"Those are the doctors and nurses who are on my team. They make their rounds every morning and talk about how I'm doing and what's going to happen next. Did you sleep at all last night? Your hair looks ridiculous."

I try to answer her question through a huge yawn.

"I finally fell asleep really early this morning." I run my fingers through my hair, trying to tame it. "How do you sleep at night? There were nurses in and out all night long."

"I get some sleep during the day, too, so it all works out."

"I'm glad I don't have to go to school today—I'm still really tired. I'm gonna find some coffee."

"Bring me some!"

Chapter Twelve

Miranda is true to her word. During the next few weeks, she keeps a very strict schedule of visitors. She creates an online spreadsheet and shares it with every single person in our class. And I mean *every*. Somehow, Miranda got her hands on the class directory from the administrator's office. There's a lot more information in that directory than you can find in the yearbook—address, phone numbers, e-mail, even social security numbers!

"Miranda!" I exclaim when she shows me the list. "How the hell did you get this?"

"I have a few useful connections," she replies. Her grin is positively wicked.

"You're not going to do anything with these social security numbers, are you?" I'm terrified that she might start stealing identities and open a bunch of credit cards in the names of unsuspecting students.

"No, goofball. I just want to make sure that I have a complete list. And, look," she's pointing at the tablet "There's a column for extra-curriculars, so it'll be easy to sort by the track team, the football team…"

"Oh, and by the clubs, too!" I'm starting to see the value in this. Miranda keeps scrolling down the list—it feels like it will never end.

"How many kids are in our class?" I ask her. "Over 1,000, right?"

"Yup! Exactly 1,251."

So, with a very detailed list of 1,251 students to choose from, Angie pretty much has visitors every day. She spends hours with the football players playing Scrabble, and when the Show Choir visits, they play Fortnite.

There are some days when she's just too tired and sick to do anything. Connor comes to see her one Saturday, and she has a hard time holding a conversation. After about 20 minutes, she needs to take a nap.

"Did I do something wrong?" asks Connor, as I walk him down the hall.

"Oh, god, no," I tell him. "Why would you think that?"

"I don't know." He stuffs his hands in the pockets of his jeans. He's looking down at the floor, like he doesn't want to meet my eyes.

"I feel like I'm not doing enough for her," he says.

We're walking very slowly through the reception area, toward the elevators. There's a huge picture window to my left—I notice that the sun is just starting to set. In a few days the time will change, and it will be pitch-black by 5:30.

"I feel like that, too."

Connor's eyes widen in surprise.

"You?" he exclaims. "But you're here all the time! I think the only people who are here more are Angie's parents."

"But I'm still doing all the things I want to do. I go to track practice after school, and I go to the meets on the weekend."

It's hard for me to discuss how I feel about this. The guilt is crushing sometimes, especially because I'm still doing something that I know Angie loves so much. And she can't do it. Connor is the only person I share the feeling with, mostly because I think he'll understand.

"I think it's probably good that you're still running track. And aren't other people here like all the time?"

I know he's right. I still feel that I never spend enough time with Angie, but maybe I'm being too hard on myself.

"Yeah," I reply. "Miranda is really good about that."

Connor leans his head back and lets out a kind of grunting sigh.

"This whole thing sucks. I know she's gonna get better, but how long is it going to take?"

"I wish I knew," I whisper.

Angie is about two weeks into the month-long treatment when Halloween arrives, which really sucks. We shouldn't be celebrating our favorite holiday in the hospital. I go ahead and buy a Mommy Shark and Baby Shark costume from Amazon so we're able to have our matching costumes.

The nurses on Angie's floor decorate the doors with spiders and bats. Purple and black lights are strung along the top of the station, and there's some pumpkin carving happening in the playroom. I notice that they aren't real pumpkins—they're the foam ones that don't have any nasty guts that need to be cleaned out.

The chemo is affecting Angie pretty much like Carrie said it will. She feels pukey, and her hair is starting to fall out in clumps. Before we get dressed in our costumes, Angie asks if I would do a favor for her. She hands me a set of hair clippers and points to her head.

"My hair started falling out and I just want to cut it all off. I need you to do it for me."

She leads the way into the bathroom. I follow.

I use the hospital-issue clippers to shave her head. We stand together in front of the small mirror in the cramped bathroom, and I run the blades across her skull. I think she might start to cry, but she doesn't. I know that I would have, if I were her.

We gaze at each other in the mirror. She looks so young without any hair. And small. All of her gorgeous, dark hair is in a small pile around our feet.

"It's just hair," says Angie. "It's going to grow back."

I really like my hair and I would have tried to hold onto it as long as I possibly could.

"You're handling this better than I would be," I tell her.

"Well, you know. I'd rather lose my hair than my life. So...."

I am stunned. I know that I've been hanging out in the hospital with my best friend while she's been going through cancer treatment for the last two weeks, but I think I forgot how serious it really is.

Angie turns around and looks straight in my eyes.

"A little two-year-old girl died this morning. She had leukemia, too. I don't know all the details, but I saw her mom crying, and I heard the nurses talking about it. I don't think they even realized that I was there. This is real, Cassidy. This is serious. I'd be happy to be bald for the rest of my life, if it means that I'll have a life."

She turns back to the mirror and runs a hand over her smooth scalp.

"All righty," she says. "Where's my Mommy Shark costume? Let's go trick-or-treat!"

I actually brought a Costco-sized bag of candy because I knew that there would be lots of kids looking for a handout. Angie pulls the pink costume over her head. It's a one-piece, and her face peeks out of the Mommy Shark's mouth. She looks like she's ten.

The hallway is filled with tiny Spidermen and Wonder Women. There is one cowboy, and an itty-bitty Baby Shark who pushes her IV pole right up to us and starts singing, "Do do do do do!"

Her little hand is clutching a plastic pumpkin bucket, and I drop a handful of candy in it. I don't see any reason to give her only one or two.

"What do you say, Maia?" asks her dad, who is standing a few steps behind her.

"Do do do do do do!"

And she's off to ask the next person she sees for treats.

Angie is having a blast giving candy to all of the kiddoes trick-or-treating up and down her hallway. She starts the evening standing just outside the door to her room. All the kids know that Angie's pink costume is Mommy Shark, and my yellow one is Baby Shark. Of course, they all have to sing to us. It's pretty dang cute.

After about thirty minutes, Angie asks me to find a chair for her. I look at her face, and I realize that I should have checked on her earlier. She looks exhausted. Her face is pale—her beautiful golden, Latinx skin is nowhere to be seen. The lids are heavy over her sunken eyes. She can hardly keep them open.

I bring the small visitor's chair from her room out to the hallway. She lowers herself gingerly into the chair. Her shark costume poofs up into her face and she flattens it back down with her hands. The bowl of candy on her lap almost takes a tumble, but I dive for it, and I'm able to catch it.

"Are you okay? Do you need the nurse?"

"No, I'm just a little tired. It's fine. I'll probably be ready to go to bed soon, but I want to hand out candy a little longer."

A little longer ends up being just about ten minutes before Angie is done. I know that she tries hard to stay awake, but exhaustion is overtaking her. Then she does need the nurse to help her to bed.

"Angie, are you having trouble standing?" Rachel asks as she bends over Angie to help her. She had started her shift about fifteen minutes earlier. I see her place two fingers on Angie's wrist.

"I just feel really tired all of a sudden. I think I need to go to bed."

"All right, honey. Your pulse is normal. Let's get you into bed, and then I'll get your evening meds."

Rachel helps Angie stand and they shuffle slowly back into the hospital room, toward the bed. There are still a few trick-or-treaters in the hallway. I stand in the doorway with the chair, not quite knowing what I should do. Should I hand out some more candy, or go into Angie's room with her? I decide that a good compromise is to leave our leftover candy with the nurses. They can either give it to the kiddoes who are still running up and down the hallway, or enjoy some of it themselves.

I scoot the chair back to its original spot and look at Angie and Rachel. Angie is already snoozing—I figure that's my cue to leave.

Rachel is still busy with medication and the IV pole. She's trying to stop the beeping, but the display keeps saying, "Air In Line."

"I'm going to take off now," I tell her. "Angie's sleeping."

"Oh, okay, honey! You have a good night," Rachel calls as I walk out the door.

Chapter Thirteen

On November sixteenth, Angie is scheduled for a bone marrow biopsy. This is a test to see if the chemo is doing what it's supposed to be doing. Apparently, the leukemia should be completely gone at this point. At least, that's what the doctors told Angie and her parents. There should be "an undetectable amount" of bad cells in her bone marrow.

It's now the nineteenth, and I have yet to hear any news. I'm getting ready to visit Angie, to find out if she knows anything yet.

Mom is in the middle of planning our Thanksgiving dinner, which is only a week away. I think she enjoys planning the meal as much as she enjoys preparing it. We always have about twenty people at our table. Or, I should probably say tables, since we don't have one table that can fit everyone. Mom always invites her friends for Thanksgiving. They have all known each other for years—some friends are from work, and some go all the way back to college at the University of Colorado.

They've seen each other through marriage, babies being born, and several divorces. Mom's best friend, Janey, even lost her husband in a really bad accident about ten years ago. He had been riding his bicycle, practicing for a triathlon. He was totally into running races all the time. He had competed in some shorter distance triathlons, but this was going to be his first Ironman and he was totally pumped. Even though I was only six at the time, I remember it.

We had been planning to travel to Oklahoma with them—that's where the race was. He was going to have the best cheer team! Me, Mom, Janey, and their son, Evan. We were making posters with sayings like, "Run like zombies are chasing you!" and "Faster, Faster!" I remember pouring purple glitter all over the letters and being so proud of how pretty that sign was.

And then, one morning Mom came to me in tears and told me that we didn't need the posters anymore. Janey's husband had been hit by a speeding Land Rover while he was on his bicycle. The asshole wasn't even drinking—he was just an asshole who didn't want to share the road with a cyclist.

So now Janey and Evan, along with Mom's other friends, join us for most holidays.

We always do a potluck on Thanksgiving—Mom says it makes the whole thing easier for her, but I don't buy it. Mom still prepares a ton of food. She always cooks the turkey on the grill, so she can have oven space for bread, sweet potatoes, dressing, and a dozen other carb-filled side dishes.

I usually help out by baking a couple of pies and then cleaning up with the other kids. I've tried for years to get Mom to use paper plates so clean-up can be easier, but she absolutely refuses. She wouldn't even use paper napkins—all of the waste is bad for the environment. So I'm stuck doing a mountain of dishes every Thanksgiving, along with three or four other kids. But, honestly, I don't really mind. It actually goes pretty fast, and we all get to snack on the leftovers.

As I come downstairs to head to the hospital Mom is sitting at the kitchen table, writing her menu in a small notebook. I know that she's also writing a schedule of when she'll start cooking and a shopping list.

"Cassie, what kind of pies are you making this year?" she asks me, without looking up from her list.

I grin, because I had actually been thinking about what I want to bake.

"I really want to do a lemon meringue," I reply, as I pull on a jacket. I'm about to head over to the hospital. "And a pumpkin, because a lot of people like pumpkin. But I'm excited about the lemon meringue."

Now she looks up at me.

"That's more of a spring-time pie and not really Thanksgiving-ish, don't you think?"

"It doesn't matter—it's going to be totally delicious! All creamy, with the perfect balance between tart and sweet. And the meringue will be golden brown." I'm doing my best to convince her.

"Hmmmm…that does sound pretty good." And I notice her add lemons and eggs to the list. "Are you going to the hospital, honey?"

"Yeah, I'm hoping that Angie has some news about the biopsy. It's been a few days. I would think she would have heard something by now."

She tears a page out of her notebook.

"On your way back can you swing by Whole Foods and pick up a few things for me?" Mom asks, as she hands me the list.

"Sure, I can do that. See you later!"

As I drive to the hospital the skies become more and more grey and the clouds look heavy, as if they're ready to drop an ocean of rain onto Dallas. The temperature is still in the low 60s, but colder temperatures are forecast for later in the night.

I swing through the Whataburger drive-through again to pick up several orders of fries for the two of us to munch on.

I'm in a great mood as I enter the elevator and push the button for Angie's floor. The last time I saw her, she was looking really good. She had more energy, and her face had a little more color. We spent a few hours playing Super Mario, and she wasn't tired. I'm really optimistic about the biopsy results. I'm sure that the leukemia is practically gone.

But when I walk into Angie's room, I'm met with Angie lying in her bed working in a Sudoku book, and the two ladies from Carter Bloodcare are back. Netflix is on the TV with the sound muted and captions on. *New Girl* is playing—Angie and I watched every season so many times, that we don't even need captions to know what's going on. The only sound is the pheresis machine, whirring away. The catheter protrudes from Angie's neck.

"What the hell happened?" I blurt out, before I can think of anything constructive to say.

Angie gives me a smile. "It's time for Plan B. Hey, are those French fries?"

My heart sinks. "I suppose that means the biopsy wasn't great."

"Yeah, I still had around thirty percent leukemia cells."

I climb onto the bed next to her.

"Oh, Angie," I sigh. I have no words. All I can think to say is, "That sucks." But, to my surprise, when she starts answering me, she doesn't sound as devastated as I feel.

"It's okay. Plan B is this immunotherapy that's really cool. They're collecting my T cells, then they're going to modify them in a lab so they attack my leukemia cells. They'll put them back in my bloodstream through my port."

I vaguely remember when Carrie explained that whole process to us.

"You don't sound too worried," I tell her.

"Nah, it's going to be fine. It'll take about a month until the new cells are ready, so I'll stay in here. They're going to keep me on chemo so the leukemia doesn't get any worse."

At that moment Carrie walks through the door to check on the pheresis progression. Her blonde hair is piled on top of her head today.

"Hi there ladies!" she greets us. She's her usual perky self. I wonder if it's an act, or if she really is this upbeat all the time. "We've got some excitement happening today."

She walks over to the side of Angie's bed and examines the tube that's protruding from her neck.

"It looks good. Are you in any pain, honey?"

"No, it's fine. How much longer?"

Carrie glances at the bag that's collecting the deep-red, thick liquid.

"I think we're getting close. Probably about an hour left." Carrie turns back to face Angie. "So, I heard that you're stuck here for another month, until your cells are ready."

"Yeah, that's what they told me." Angie makes direct eye contact with me before she says, "But I'm pretty sure that someone will bring Thanksgiving dinner to me, so I don't miss it."

Well, of course I'm planning to do that already. Angie would kill for my mom's chunky, homemade cranberry sauce. She always puts in apples and orange peel with the cranberries, which adds an amazing flavor to the sauce.

"Carrie," I ask, "Why does Angie have to stay here? Why can't she go home?"

"That's a great question. Right now, her immune system is very suppressed. She wouldn't be able to fight off any type of infection or virus. Angie has a much better chance of staying safe if she just stays here."

Geez, it seems like every time I ask something, whichever doctor or nurse is there would say, "That's a great question." It's kind of patronizing. Whether or not the question is "great" doesn't matter. Just tell me the answer!

"Can she still have visitors?" I hope so. Angie loves when all of our friends visit.

"Of course! The more the merrier." Her eyes travel toward the bags that I'm still clutching. "I thought something smelled yummy. You should dig in before those fries get cold."

She's right—I completely forgot about them. Angie drops the Sudoku book on her lap and is reaching for the Whataburger bags. As she's leaning forward, one of the Carter Bloodcare ladies jump up from her chair and rushes over to her.

"Honey, be careful! These tubes don't reach very far!" She takes one of the bags from me and hands it to Angie.

To me, it looks like Angie can definitely stand to eat a few more meals. Or maybe a few pints of Blue Bell Cookies and Cream.

Angie digs in like a starving woman.

"Hospital food gets old after a while," she explains.

"Yeah, I bet it does." I reply.

I look closely at my friend. I've been with her almost every day since her diagnosis and since she was admitted to the hospital, so it makes sense that I don't notice the changes that are taking place in her body. I bring her fries and homework, we watch Netflix, and I catch her up on the gossip at school.

But now that I really look at her, I realize how weak and small she looks. It isn't her hair loss—she's actually rocking the smooth scalp. What stands out to me is how thin she looks. The fire that always shines so bright in her eyes is much dimmer. My spicy little friend, who always wins any race she runs, is fading before me, like that photograph of Marty McFly and his family. My face must have given my thoughts away.

"Cassidy, is something wrong?"

I shake my head and come back to the present.

"No, no," I lie. "I was just thinking about Thanksgiving. My mom wants me to pick up a few things from the store.

"Girl, you are totally bringing me Thanksgiving dinner. Especially that cranberry sauce."

"Of course! And I'll bring Connor, too!" I wiggle my eyebrows at her.

Surprisingly, she shakes her head and says, "Oh,

no, you don't have to do that."

"Wait, what?" The last time Connor visited he had expressed some worry, but I thought everything was okay between the two of them, and that they're still a couple.

"Did something happen?" I ask.

"No, nothing like that. I just…." She pauses for a moment, as if she's struggling to find the right words. "I just don't feel very attractive right now. Not only because of my hair, but I know I've lost a lot of weight. And the chemo makes my brain so fuzzy—it's hard for me to follow what he's saying sometimes, and then I feel stupid."

Well, shit. How am I supposed to respond to this? I'm glad that she feels she can talk to me, but I have no idea what to say to make her feel better. That is all I really want to do.

But, honestly, can anybody say anything to make Angie feel better? She's in an incredibly crappy situation. Here she is, a beautiful, talented girl getting ready to start fielding college scholarship offers, and then this just slams into her like a runaway bus. It isn't fair. I know, I know. Nobody ever told me that life would be fair. But this *really* isn't fair. I don't think anyone could come up with the right words to make my friend forget this hell she's going through and feel good about the world.

I scoot closer to her on the bed. Carrie had discretely left the room a minute earlier, but the Carter Bloodcare ladies are still here. I pretend that Angie and I are alone in that sterile room, and I tell her what's in my heart.

"Oh, honey. I don't know what I can say to make you feel better. Cancer sucks. It shouldn't have happened to you. Especially not you, because you're the best! This won't last forever. You'll finish your treatment, and you'll have your gorgeous hair and body back again, and you'll be the smartest chick in school. I'm so sorry that you're sad."

She holds her arms out to me and we hug for a long minute.

Chapter Fourteen

I'm just about to turn the corner into my neighborhood, when my phone rings. My mom's picture appears on the screen.

"Hey Mom, what's up?" I say as I answer her call.

"Hi sweetheart! I just wanted to make sure you were still able to swing by Whole Foods and get the things on my list. I really need to start working on that cranberry sauce now. And I have a few additions to the list I gave you this morning."

Dammit, I totally spaced that I needed to pick up her groceries. Whole Foods is on the other side of town. I'm not even close. But I promised and don't want to say no to my mom.

"Sure, but it'll take a little while. Can you text me the new list?"

A few minutes later, Mom's updated shopping list shows up on my phone. In addition to cranberry sauce fixings, she needs coconut milk, mushrooms, and tahini. Sounds like she's making her vegan cream of mushroom soup. Fine by me! That's some good stuff. I can bring some to Angie the next day, too.

Ten minutes later I pull into the crowded grocery store parking lot. Whole Foods is always crowded, even at night. On my way into the store I grab a carry-basket. I'm not buying much, so that'll be fine. Of course, I have a couple of reusable shopping bags with me.

I grab the mushrooms first, because I entered the store at the produce section. Mom always uses gorgeous baby portabellas for the soup, so that's what I choose. Next, on to the plant-based beverage aisle.

I'm turning into the aisle when I have a near collision with a woman pushing her kid in a shopping cart. The boy is about three years old, and he has a terrible cough. It sounds like he's hacking up a lung. I feel a few drops of his saliva actually make contact with me. Effing nasty!

"Excuse me," his mother says to me.

"Is your son okay?" I ask her.

"Oh, he'll be fine." And she pushes him toward produce.

I sure hope he will be. I pick up the coconut milk and begin looking for the tahini. Tahini usually comes in a jar. It's a paste made from ground sesame seeds. But employees at various grocery stores around Richardson can't seem to agree on where it belongs in the store. Sometimes it's in the Asian food section, and once I found it in the Jewish food section. I know it's in the store somewhere, but it will take a little time to hunt it down.

Finally, I find it in the produce section. It's the kind

that needs to be refrigerated.

I make it to the checkout with my basket of goodies. Of course, the shelves at the checkout are full of tempting, tasty things. I grab a bar of German dark chocolate infused with chili pepper, then pay for my groceries.

I notice the woman with the coughing boy in the checkout lane next to me. He's still hacking up that lung, and now I notice that he looks really hot. His face is red and shiny. He looks like he might pass out in the shopping cart. His mom better get him home and put him to bed. Geez, I hope he's not contagious.

I pay quickly and make my way back to my sweet Elsa.

Chapter Fifteen

Miranda calls me as I'm driving home from the store. I think that's odd; she normally hates talking to anyone on the phone and only talks to people by texting. I've seen her ignore so many calls from people she knows.

I answer the phone—she's talking so fast and is so excited, I can hardly understand what she's trying to tell me. All I heard is, "Blah blah blah blah, $10,000!"

Her excitement is contagious, but I still don't know what she's talking about.

"Miranda, you need to slow down! I can't understand a word you're saying."

I hear her take a few breaths to calm herself. Then she says, "The GoFundMe for Angie's family is more than $10,000!"

I don't think I heard her right. Did Miranda say the

STUCK

GoFundMe has over $10,000?

"What?" I squawk into the phone. "$10,000? How did you raise that much money?"

"I was all over Facebook, Instagram, Twitter, and TikTok. I shared the crap out of Angie's story and the GoFundMe link." She pauses to catch her breath. "I withdrew all the money today, and I'm going to bring it to her parents. There's a cashier's check burning a hole in my pocket. Come with me!"

"Right now?" After my trip to Whole Foods I'm hungry. But that's okay—I can swing by a drive-thru on the way to pick up Miranda. I check the time on my phone. "I can be there in about half an hour. Want anything from Chick-Fil-A?"

"Of course I do! Bring me a twelve-pack of nuggets, fries, and a lemonade."

Geez, she must be starving! But I have no problem getting a meal for her. I'm amazed that she's able to raise so much money for Angie's parents. I feel a bit guilty—I should have been the one raising money and slamming social media. All I do is sit in Angie's hospital room and bring her pastries.

I pull into the driveway of our house and drop off the groceries Mom asked for.

"I'm going out again, Mom!" I call as I run back out the front door. "I won't be too late!"

I pull into Miranda's driveway and grab the two bags of Chick-Fil-A as I hop out of the car. The house is brightly lit by solar spotlights that are strategically placed in the garden. It isn't a brand-new house, or a fancy house, but I can tell that her family takes care of it. They always have—I remember that from when we were friends years ago.

I ring the high-tech video doorbell. After a

moment Miranda's voice comes through the speaker.

"Give me a minute! I'll be down in a sec."

I hear footsteps from the other side of the door, and then it swings wide.

"Mmmmm…that smells so good!" she says as she steps aside to let me in. We walk into the kitchen and unpack our dinner.

Miranda dunks a nugget into buffalo sauce and takes a long pull on her lemonade straw.

"Do Angie's parents know we're coming over?" I ask as I bite into a waffle fry. Pretty good, but couldn't hold a candle to Whataburger fries.

"Yeah, I called them a little while ago." She pauses while she munches on another nugget. "I have an idea that I'm thinking about doing."

"Oh, yeah? What's that?"

"Well, all of this stuff with Angie is kind of bringing up what my family went through when my brother had cancer. I didn't understand back then, because I was little. But now I realize that a lot of people helped us. They didn't have GoFundMe back then, but so many people brought us food and I think someone at my dad's work started a collection. I don't know how much money they raised, but I'm sure every little bit helped. They both were out of work for a while."

She pauses to eat some more Chick-Fil-A. I stay quiet, because it feels like Miranda isn't done talking yet. I have the feeling that she's opening up about something that she's never spoken about before.

"So, this idea I've been thinking about—it's kind of a foundation to honor my little brother and to help other kids who are going through cancer treatment. I'm not exactly sure what I want to do, but I want to do something."

"Oh, Miranda," I start. I am just astonished by this girl—no, this woman—who's becoming my friend again. The thoughts that bloom in her brain will never show up in mine. I don't know how she gets her inspirations, but I'm glad she's sharing them with me. "I think that's a great idea. It's a wonderful way to remember your brother."

"Yeah, that's what I thought! I don't have it all figured out yet, but I really feel like I should do something. I hate that we never talk about him." She quickly clears our empty bags off the table and puts them in the trash can. Her purse is hanging on the back of one of the dining chairs—she opens it and looks inside, then says, "Okay, the check is here. I didn't lose it. Let's go!"

We all live within a few blocks of each other so it doesn't take long for Elsa to transport us to Angie's house. It's almost nine-thirty, and I'm a little worried that we'll be getting there a little too late. But when we pull up in front of the house, all of the windows are blazing with light.

We ring the doorbell and knock on the front door, but there's no answer; it sounds like a raging party is going on inside, so I'm not surprised that no one can hear us. The door is unlocked—we walk inside.

There are about twelve people gathered in the kitchen and everyone is talking and laughing loudly. Nobody notices us for a few seconds. They're all eating lasagna; there are two big pans sitting on the kitchen table.

Miranda and I are standing at the edge of the party, not really wanting to interrupt. Finally, Mrs. Gutiérrez notices us. She sets her plate down on the counter and rushes over to us, a huge smile on her face and her arms wide open. I expect to be wrapped in a hug, but instead of me, she grabs Miranda and holds her tight.

"Everyone! Everyone, listen!" she calls, as she turns back to the group. One arm is around Miranda's shoulders, and they both face everybody who's gathered in the kitchen.

"This is Miranda! This is the young woman who organized this wonderful Meal Train. I haven't had to cook since Angie got sick. Three or four times a week somebody brings us dinner. Thank you, Miranda."

Mrs. Gutiérrez pronounces her name "Mee-rahn-da." I might start doing that.

The group claps and cheers for her—Mrs. Gutiérrez gives her a kiss on the cheek.

"Oh, it's nothing, Mrs. Gutiérrez. I'm just glad it worked out. Sometimes, people don't want to sign up to be on a Meal Train, but this was easy. A lot of people really care about Angie." She reaches into her purse and pulls out the cashier's check. "I have something else for your family. I started a GoFundMe when Angie first got sick. We were able to raise just over $10,000. So, here, this is for you."

Miranda hands the check to Angie's mother—but she doesn't take it right away.

"What?" she asks. She looks at the check and then at Miranda's face. "That can't be right. Ten thousand dollars?"

"Yes, that's right."

"Mrs. Gutiérrez," I begin, "Miranda shared Angie's story all over social media and asked a lot of people to contribute. She's really good at that kind of thing. And so many people really care about Angie and you."

She's silent and looks from me to Miranda several

times. Then she bursts into tears and grabs both of us in a huge hug. The room erupts in cheers and loud applause. Mrs. Gutiérrez is crying and laughing at the same time.

"Girls, come sit down. Eat some lasagna—we have so much. Come on." She steers us to the table and gently forces us to sit down. Someone else places plates and silverware in front of us, and before we know it, Mrs. Gutiérrez places a big piece of cheesy, saucy lasagna on each plate.

Miranda and I look at each other and I know she's thinking what I'm thinking. We are both still full from our nuggets and fries. But we don't want to insult Mrs. Gutiérrez. We pick up our forks and dig in.

Chapter Sixteen

Three Months Earlier

It was the last weekend before our junior year would begin. On a hot Saturday night in mid-August, it didn't feel like school was about to start in a few days. It feels like summer would go on indefinitely—that we could wear our cutoffs and tank tops forever.

Connor, Angie's new maybe-boyfriend, said we should show up at another kid's house for a party. I didn't even know this boy, but Connor did, so it was okay. His house was in the newer area of town, where all of the McMansions were built. The entire neighborhood was behind an iron gate and we needed to type a code into a keypad.

I turned to Angie. "Do you have the code?" I ask.

"Oh, yeah, I think Connor messaged it to me. Let me check."

She scrolled through her texts until she found what she was looking for.

"Got it! Try 664433."

I punched the buttons on the keypad, and the massive gate began sliding slowly to the right.

"Good thing it worked!" I exclaimed. "Otherwise we would have had to find something else to do tonight."

I steered Elsa through the twisty streets while Angie read me the directions on her navigation app. Every house in this neighborhood was massive—so were the lots they were sitting on. It looked like they were all at least an acre, but I wasn't sure. I just knew that the front and back yards were all much bigger than any other I've seen in town. They were all illuminated by bright up-lights that made them really stand out in the darkness. The sun had set about an hour ago.

Once we found the right street it was easy to find the house—a ton of cars were parked in the driveway, along the sidewalk, and half of a BMW was parked on the lawn. That couldn't be good for the grass—my dad would have been pissed about something like that.

I parked about a half block away from the house. We threw our purses in the trunk, locked it up, and I put my keys in the front pocket of my shorts. Angie and I had agreed long ago that when we went to a party, there was no need to bring a purse in the house. It was just a nuisance that we needed to keep track of, and we wanted no part of that.

As we walked up the long sidewalk to the front door, we could hear the sounds of the party coming from the backyard. A hand-written sign taped to the front door instructed us to follow the path around to the back.

The sounds of loud music and laughter greeted us as we opened the gate and stepped into the huge garden area. The backyard was packed with a lot of people I recognized and even more that I didn't. Angie must have been thinking the same thing, because she yelled in my ear, "I don't know most of the people here! How are we going to find Connor?"

"I guess we just walk around until we see him," I shouted.

String lights were hung all through the large yard. An in-ground pool was smack-dab in the middle. It was beautifully landscaped with oak trees and colorful flower beds. One of them was full of zinnias—I knew about those, because my mom planted them every year. She loved how colorful they were, and during the summer there was always a vase full of them in the kitchen. She would love the landscaping in this yard. But I didn't see any pumpkins or tomatillos, like Angie's mom grew.

We made our way to the patio. There was a steady stream of people going in and out of the house. I was surprised to see that above the patio was a deck, and the door leading into the house didn't lead into the kitchen, like most homes in the area. Instead, people were streaming in and out of what looked like a walk-out basement. A walk-out basement? Those are few and far between in Texas. Nobody had a basement. I think it had something to do with the Texas soil. These people must be rolling in the dough, to have a McMansion with a basement.

From out of nowhere, a blond guy handed us each a red Solo cup.

"Ladies, you need some libations!" He kissed Angie on the cheek, turned around, and kind of danced away.

We were both laughing, and I asked her if she knew that boy.

"No, I've never seen him before!"

I looked into the cup, wondering what the blond kisser had brought us. It was beer, of course. Cheap, watery, light beer. While I enjoyed sharing my dad's Shiner with him occasionally, I knew that I didn't want to drink this nasty stuff.

I set the cup down on the nearest table, without really noticing where I was placing it. When I did, a group of kids began shouting at me and telling me to, "Move the damn cup!" They were in the middle of a beer pong game, so I really didn't see the problem.

"Hey, it's just another cup of beer!" I explained. I retrieved the cup and added it to the last row, evening out the spacing. "See, it's perfect!"

"All right!" This was from the guy holding the ping pong ball. He was smiling and ready to start playing. I recognized him from my Biology class—a big, nice guy who always had a smile on his face. He tossed the ball into one of the cups—the group that was gathered around the table threw up their hands and gave a loud cheer.

My eyes scanned the crowd, searching for Angie. We had a deal that whenever we went to a party we didn't have to stay together the whole time, but I always made sure I knew where she was, and she did the same for me. Last year at a house party a senior named Cinna had been with three of her girlfriends. She disappeared, and the friends didn't think to look for her. They just said they had no idea where she had gone, and they even thought she might have left early. None of them ever considered checking on her.

Cinna had been roofied by a boy from another school, who she didn't know. She left her drink alone for less than a minute, which was more than enough time for the sleaze-ball to sprinkle the powder in her cup. Then he took her upstairs to one of the bedrooms.

She never specifically said what happened, and never blamed the boy or filed charges. But we knew. Angie and I talked about it a lot—how Cinna used to be a lot more outgoing and chatty. Since the party, she seemed to have shrunk inside herself, trying to disappear.

What we didn't understand was how could she have been at this party with friends, and then they just left her? If they came to the party together, they should have left together! That made no sense at all. That was when Angie and I promised each other that we would always make sure we knew where the other one was.

I didn't know Cinna, but I knew who she was. She was all about her make-up and clothes—I had the impression that there was nothing more important to her than the way she looked. She had the blonde, flippy pony-tail, and super-long lash extensions. We would say hi to each other when we passed in the hallway, but I never went out of my way to talk to her.

A few weeks after the party incident, Cinna and I happened to be in Ms. Malone's classroom together. We had both been recruited to help decorate the room for the holidays. The theme was *The Gift of The Magi*— Ms. Malone always decorated her room based on a theme. The year before it had been *A Christmas Carol*, and people were supposed to create their own version of one of the Christmas ghosts. The favorite, by far, had been the Ghost of Christmas Future.

This year's assignment was to write our own version of *The Gift of The Magi*. What would we be willing to give up for someone we loved?

So Cinna and I were decorating the classroom with elaborately decorated gift boxes.

We worked in silence for a while—honestly, I didn't know what to say to her, and we had never been friends. And then she broke the silence.

"You know, I always wished I had a close friend like you have Angie."

That's a surprise. "But, you have lots of friends, Cinna. You're always with a group."

"They're not real friends. It's not like what you guys have. You really care about each other. You look out for each other." She gave me a small smile. "That's special."

What happened to Cinna at that party really freaked out Angie and me. We wanted to go to parties, and we definitely wanted to make sure nothing like that ever happened to us. So we came up with our system.

I spotted Angie over by the pool, talking to Connor. Good, I thought. I was glad that she found him. I moved a little closer to her, just until we made eye contact. We smiled at each other and nodded—we had a way of being able to talk to each other without saying a word.

I decided to hang out with the beer pong group. They seemed fun, and the guy from my Biology class kept smiling at me. I took a few turns tossing the ping pong ball into the cups, and I didn't do too badly. Most of the time I was not the one who had to drink—and when I did have to, I just pretended. I dumped the contents of the cup in a potted jasmine plant that was right behind me. I refused to drink that nastiness.

All of a sudden we heard a shout from above us. It sounded like someone called out, "Cannonbaaaalllll!" as if they were jumping into the pool. And then something—or someone?—seemed to fly in an arc from the deck above me and splashed into the pool. An enormous amount of water sloshed over the side, high into the air. Everyone who was within ten feet of the edge of the pool was drenched.

Did someone really just do a cannonball off the deck into the pool? I peered into the water and saw a guy wearing only his boxer-briefs swimming to the surface. The crowd was cheering, urging him to, "Do that again, dude!"

But before he had the chance to get out of the pool, a loud voice boomed over the cheers of the crowd and even the loud music streaming from the Bluetooth speakers. It came from the deck, from where the cannonballer had jumped.

"What the hell is going on here? Turn off that music! Braaaadyyyy!" This was the voice of a very pissed off dad. But at least now we knew whose house we were at—Brady's.

Angie appeared next to me. "I think that's our cue," she said, as she grabbed my hand and led me out the back gate. I turned to wave good-bye to Biology guy and he waved back and shot me a million dollar smile.

Chapter Seventeen

For the next week, I divide my time between visiting Angie and helping my mom prepare for Thanksgiving dinner. School's out for the entire week of Thanksgiving, which is fantastic. I sleep in, go for a run, help Mom a bit with food prep, then go to hang out with Angie.

On Thanksgiving Day the house is packed full of Mom's friends, as I knew it would be. All the usual suspects are there, including Janey and Evan. But there are also some new faces, which makes for very lively conversation around the table.

I'm helping with finishing touches—pouring the gravy into the boat and mashing some cream into the potatoes. All of a sudden, I feel the urge to clear my throat—it's feeling a bit scratchy. Suddenly, the throat clearing turns into a full-blown coughing fit. I throw my face into the crook of my elbow. I know how to do the vampire cough, so my germs don't go flying every-where. It takes a minute to recompose myself, but then I'm fine.

Chairs are packed around our eight-foot-long table, and there's hardly any room for passing around all of the serving dishes. I sit around the kitchen island with Evan and two other kids—they are both a bit younger than me, and it's the first time I've seen them at our table. I keep hopping up to grab the mashed potatoes, or the green bean salad from the "grown-up table," so the newcomers won't feel awkward.

I've just grabbed the balsamic-glazed Brussels sprouts, when I hear someone raise their voice. I hear it very clearly above the din of the other conversations—it is high-pitched and shrill.

"Beth, do you mean to tell me that you're one of those anti-vaxxers?"

I decide to tune into this conversation. What my dad had told me about the early days of their marriage and their differences in parenting styles has stayed with me. I've never really been exposed to both sides of this argument, and I want to hear what both people have to say.

"You bet I am," is Mom's reply. "And I'm proud of it! I don't understand how anyone can be in favor of injecting all of these toxins into a child's body, especially with all of the damage they cause. It's the same reason that I won't get a flu shot—the medical and pharmaceutical industries are just trying to make money off of the public."

Another voice chimes in.

"Well, Beth, I'm not so sure that vaccines and flu shots are big money-makers. One vaccine costs about $30, no matter what disease it's protecting you against.

I think it's treating people who get the diseases that costs the most money."

The speaker, who must have been the mother of one or both of the new kids at the island, turns to her companion.

"Where was that case of tetanus that happened a year or so ago? Somewhere in the Pacific Northwest, right?"

"Yes, I remember that!" someone across the table says. "A little boy, maybe six or seven-years-old, fell down and got a cut. The parents treated him at home— they even sutured it themselves!"

Oh, gag. That is nasty. I would never let my mom or dad stitch up a cut.

"Anyway," she continues, "a few days later he was crying uncontrollably, and he couldn't open his mouth. You know, lock-jaw is one of the first symptoms."

Heads nod around the table.

"They air lifted him to a hospital where he spent over 40 days in ICU. That cost around $800,000! That's what's expensive, not the vaccine."

"Oh, I heard that story," my mom cuts in. "The parents just didn't clean the wound well enough. If they had, that never would have happened. And I admire them! They stuck to their convictions and didn't let those doctors put poison in his little body."

Several heads around the table are nodding in agreement—but the look on some faces are of complete horror and disbelief.

"Why do you think vaccines are dangerous, Beth?" asks Mom's friend Janey. Her tone is calm and not at all confrontational.

"Because they all contain toxins like formaldehyde. And they cause more damage than they cure. There's no reason to pump a tiny baby's body full of all these chemicals." Mom's looking directly at her friend—I have the feeling they've probably had this conversation before.

"If they didn't cause problems," Mom continues, "then why does the CDC offer the ability to report 'adverse vaccine events?'" She makes air quotes with her fingers for the effect.

"I would think that adverse events happen sometime, but not as often as some people would like the public to believe."

Mom says nothing, but she's shaking her head.

"So, I have another question," Janey says. "Is that okay?"

I'm surprised that she asked. I think it's a good move on her part. She's not coming across as hostile—I can tell she isn't trying to slam her opinion down my mother's throat.

"Have you ever needed to go to the Emergency Room, or Urgent Care?" she asks. Then she turns in her chair to look at me. "Or, have you ever had to take Cassidy?"

Immediately, my mind goes back in time, back to when I broke my arm when I was small. I remember when she scooped me up and rushed me to the Emergency Room, so the doctor could set my arm.

I decide to butt in with my two cents.

"I had a broken arm a long time ago, and Mom took me to the doctor."

"Of course, I took Cassidy to the doctor for a broken bone. I'm not an idiot," she says, hotly. Mom's starting to get a little spicy. I think she feels attacked.

Janey's voice softens.

"Beth, I'm not calling you an idiot. You're a

vibrant, brilliant woman. And you always cook the best Thanksgiving dinner in Texas. I wouldn't want to be anywhere else. I do have another question. If you trust a doctor to treat your child in an emergency, why won't you trust him when he tells you that vaccines are safe and effective?"

"I understand why you're asking me that." Mom's starting to calm down a bit. Man, Janey is good! "And I agree—you won't find a better dinner in the state. Honestly, I just don't trust doctors, or anyone who works in the medical profession. Doctors and nurses choose that career for the money. They don't care about anyone—certainly not their patients. They all keep the best remedies, the natural ones, locked away. The medical community and big pharma are going to kill us all."

This isn't news to me. I've known for a long time that these are Mom's opinions. I've never given it much thought. When I need a sports physical for school, I just go to Urgent Care and have them take care of it. They have a consent form on file, so it's never a big deal.

"Okay, I've been trying to keep my mouth shut, but I find that comment personally insulting." This came from a woman seated two chairs away from Mom. She's a gorgeous Black woman, with killer dreadlocks. I don't recognize her—she must have come with someone else.

"I've been a nurse for fifteen years. I have personally seen the damage that this anti-vaccine and anti-science movement is causing. A young mother came in with very late stage breast cancer, because she refused chemotherapy and radiation. She thought her cancer could be healed using herbs and a raw vegetable diet. Guess what—it didn't work. Now, three small children don't have a mother. Herd immunity is real. There are people who legitimately cannot be vaccinated because of immune system issues, so they need to depend upon the rest of the population to be up to date with their own vaccines to be healthy."

All of a sudden, she turns and looks at me. "Don't you have a friend who's fighting cancer right now?"

I just nod my head. This woman is a force, and I don't want to get on her bad side.

"That's just one example of someone who is immunocompromised. Chemo and radiation wipe out any immunizations she may have had. She is very vulnerable right now."

She turns back to look at everyone at the table. "And I assure you, I am not in this career for the money. I work twelve-hour shifts, and I spend most of that time on my feet. I've been puked on and pooped on. I've seen adults and children die. It's not a glamorous job—it's an important one. I'm not in it for the money. And the vast majority of doctors and nurses that I know feel the same way that I do."

The room is completely silent—you could hear a pin drop. Even Mom is speechless.

"I look at it this way," says Janey. "It's the advancement of technology. Ten years ago, all of us here probably had some kind of flip phone, right?" Heads all around the table are nodding. "We could call or text, and that was it. We even had to use the number keys to spell out our texts. Remember that? Now, we all have either an iPhone or an Android phone. Both of them are tiny computers that we carry around in our purses and pockets all day. We watch movies on our phones. We can browse the Internet, or place an order on Amazon. They recognize our voices. We lock them with a fingerprint. We believe that they are so secure and powerful that we conduct our banking transactions with them, and we never give it a second thought. This is because we believe that the advancement of electronic technology is a good thing. We love it when a new phone is launched! Just like electronic technology, medical technology is evolving and moving forward every day. There are brilliant doctors and scientists researching cures for all kinds of diseases and ways to prevent them. We should embrace the advancement of medical technology just like we embrace the advancement of electronic technology."

Wow. That is a hell of a speech. There's some serious tension hanging in the air. I can feel it—it's like the feeling right before the sky opens up and drops buckets of rain on the city.

I feel like I have to do something to lighten the mood.

"Who's ready for some pie?" I ask. I motion to Evan and the other kids to clear some of the plates off of the main table, while I grab the smaller dessert plates from their spot on the counter, next to all of the scrumptious-looking goodies.

Dessert time is "serve yourself." As we clear the dirty dishes, all the guests begin rising and chatting to each other. When I grab a piece of pecan pie for myself, I'm thrilled to see that my lemon meringue is a hit. It seems that the few awkward moments have passed—the tension is drifting away. Sugar has that kind of positive power.

As I clear the table, I place Angie-sized portions into some of Mom's old Tupperware to take to the hospital. Angie isn't eating much these days, but I want to make sure to include as many sweet potatoes and cornbread dressing as she can handle. I fill another container with white meat and gravy.

I load the dishwasher and gobble a sweet, gooey piece of pecan pie before I get into Elsa and begin making my way to the hospital. I also grab a bottle of water from the garage fridge, in case my throat starts feeling scratchy again.

Traffic is super-light because of the holiday. I don't have to deal with the normal mess that I would have encountered at 5:30 on a non-holiday Thursday evening. The sky is slate grey and looks like it wants to snow—but the 62-degree weather has other plans. It's funny to me how the sky can be so dreary, and the air so warm. Especially in November.

As I drive, I think about that discussion that took place around the dining table and especially about the comments that the nurse made. I've been aware of my mother's opinions for years. I know that, overall, she mistrusts anyone in the medical community. I've never given that much thought, until now.

Some of the kindest, funniest, most pleasant people are the nurses in the hospital who take care of Angie all day and all night. I've seen for myself how they change her sheets every day and give her sponge baths, because she isn't supposed to take a shower. I do remember one time, when Angie was so sick from the chemo that she puked all over the bed and the floor. The nurse on duty cleaned everything up with a smile, just talking to Angie the whole time and making sure she was okay. She didn't want Angie to feel bad about the mess.

I feel the tickle in my throat again and grab the water bottle from the cup holder in the center console.

I take a sip, but it isn't helping. The tickle turns into full-blown hacking. I think I might have to pull over, but then it lets up.

I park, grab my bag of Thanksgiving goodies, and enter the hospital lobby. I check in with the concierge and they ask me the usual question.

"Any changes in your health since you were last here?"

"No, I'm fine," I tell the woman behind the counter. She hands me my sticky name tag and I make my way to the elevators.

Angie and I spend the evening eating Thanksgiving leftovers. I pull the reclining chair right next to her bed, so we can share the slice of apple pie that I brought. We take turns digging our plastic forks into the Tupperware container and shoveling the sweet, sticky bites into our mouths.

Child Life had brought DVDs of *Home Alone* and *Home Alone 2: Lost in New York*. These are classic Thanksgiving movies, of course. It's a crime to not watch the first one, at least, after the turkey has been eaten, and all the leftovers put away.

Catherine O'Hara was seated in her first-class airplane seat and was just about to scream, "Kevin!!" That's one of the best parts of the movie, and it always makes me laugh. But this time my laughter turns into another one of those damned coughing fits. I turn away from Angie, and I notice that she pauses the movie. The coughing finally stops after about thirty seconds, and I drink some water from my water bottle. I'm having a bit of a hard time catching my breath.

I look at Angie, and she's staring at me, her eyes looking worried.

"Are you okay? That didn't sound good at all."

"Yeah, I'm fine," I reply, and I drink some more water. "This just started today. I feel fine, except for this weird cough."

"Wanna keep watching the movie?"

"Yup! We're at the best part. Do you want me to get anything before you press play?"

"Yeah, some more water would be great."

I go to the kitchen area and grab a few bottles of water—I figure that I will probably need some more, too.

It's after midnight when we finish the second movie, and I'm so tired. Angie seems to have a little more energy than I do, but she agrees to turn everything off and go to sleep, too. Even if she doesn't feel like sleeping, she can read or play around on Facebook using her tablet.

My sleep is fitful—the cough wakes me several times. I struggle between not having enough covers and having too many. When I decide to give up on trying to sleep around six that morning, I am not feeling great at all. My throat is scratchy, and I feel like I might have a fever. I know it isn't good for Angie if I stay with her when I'm not feeling well.

She's still sleeping, so I grab my backpack and sneak out. In the hallway I send her a quick text, telling her to touch base with me later. As I walk through the hall and to the elevator, it feels like I'm walking a marathon. It's almost as if I'm crawling. I don't think I'll ever make it to the elevator. Finally I get there, and press the L button.

I finally make it to the lobby, but the parking garage is practically a continent away. Oh, geez, then once I get to my car, I will have to drive home. I feel so weak, that I'm not sure I'll be able to drive. What in the world is happening to me? I felt completely fine yesterday!

The parking garage elevators are in sight. Normally I take the stairs, but hell no, not today. I step inside the first car to open its doors, but then I hesitate. I can't remember which floor I parked my car on. I'm pretty sure the row is D, but is it 2D or 3D? The last thing I want to do is traipse around the uphill floors of this cavernous garage, lugging my backpack around. It feels like its weight has tripled since I left Angie's room.

Since I truly can't remember the floor number, I press the number two button and decide to start there. On the second level, I pass by rows A, B, and C, and peer down D, to see if Elsa's trunk is visible. My heart sinks when I don't see her. But I go ahead and walk down the row just to double-check. Oh, thank God, there she is hiding behind a big truck.

I open the door, throw my backpack onto the passenger seat and gratefully sink into the driver's seat. My head is now throbbing, and it feels like there are glass shards in my throat. Another sip of water helps a little, but I am still in pain.

At least I'm able to sit down. I'm completely wiped out from walking, and I just want to close my eyes. Thankfully, there won't be much traffic on the day after Thanksgiving, so it shouldn't take me long to get home. But my head is really hurting and feeling fuzzy. I back out of the parking space super-carefully and make my way down the ramp, until I come to a stop at the traffic light. I breathe a sigh of relief as I leave the parking structure.

I do my best to concentrate as I turn north onto the Dallas North Tollway and then east on 635. There are barely any other cars on the road, as I'd predicted, so it takes just about half an hour before I pull up in front of the house.

The garage door is wide open, so I know that Mom is home. I grab my backpack and begin trudging up the driveway. It feels like my pack is filled with lead bars— the slight incline of the driveway feels like I'm climbing Mt. Everest.

Climbing the stairs to my room is even harder. Somewhere from far, far away I hear my mother's voice calling my name. But it sounds like I'm far under water, she's calling me from the surface. I can't understand a thing she's saying.

"Sick," is all I can manage to say. "Bed."

"Oy wer ring blee," is what I hear her say as I walk through the open door to my room. First, I drop my backpack on the floor. I step on the heels of my shoes to take them off, then I peel off my jeans. I finally crawl under the covers and close my eyes.

I have no idea how much time goes by, but I feel my mother's hand on my forehead and hear her softly say my name.

"Cassidy, sweetie, I have some turmeric and ginger tea for you. It'll make you feel better."

I sit up slowly and take a sip of the nasty concoction. I hope she's right and that it will start making me better soon.

"Mom," I croak. Oh, god, it hurts to talk. "Throat hurts. And I'm cold. Can I have another blanket?"

"Sure, baby, I'll get you a comforter. And some honey with lemon for your throat."

"'Kay. Blanket first, Mom."

I hear her footsteps as she leaves my room. Just a couple of minutes later I feel the weight and warmth of the comforter as it floats on top of me. Then a spoon is held to my mouth. All I can do is open and let the honey and lemon mixture slide down my throat. It does feel a bit better.

Mom forces me to drink some more of that nasty-ass tea, but then she leaves me to sleep. Even with the heavy blankets, I feel cold. I figure that I'm probably running a temperature, so I reach over to my nightstand and open the drawer. There's a bottle of Tylenol stashed there, because sometimes that's the only thing that makes my joints feel better after a grueling day at the track. Mom doesn't know about it, of course. She wouldn't approve.

I swallow a couple of the capsules, using the nasty tea to wash them down. Once again, I curl up under the weight of lots of blankets and fall into a semi-restful sleep.

Chapter Eighteen

I wake to the buzzing of my phone, which I left close to my head. I open one eye just wide enough so I can see the screen. My dad's smiling face is looking at me. I kinda want to talk to him, so I press the answer button.

"Hey, Dad," I croak.

"Cassidy, what's wrong? You sound horrible." His voice is full of concern.

"I feel like crap. I'm in bed."

"Did your mom take you to the doctor?" he asks.

"No. I'm just in bed."

"Are you running a fever?"

"I think so."

"Okay, I'm coming over. I'll see you in a few minutes."

"All right, that's cool," I think I say to myself and

not my dad. My throat is really scratchy again, so I take a sip of the tea. Then I doze off again and try to fall into a real sleep.

Unfortunately, sleep is not in my near future. I hear shouting outside my door right before both of my parents, who are yelling at each other, barge into my room. I sit up in my bed and try to focus on what they're saying.

"Mark, you cannot just come in here without my permission!" That was Mom, her voice just below screaming level.

"She's my daughter too, Beth, and I'm not convinced that you're taking the best care of her." He walks quickly to my bedside and places his hand on my forehead.

"She's burning up!" Then, to my great shock and surprise, he pulls a thermometer out of his jacket pocket. It's the kind that you swipe across the forehead and the reading is instantaneous.

"Her temperature is 103.6! Beth, what the hell? You have to take her to the doctor!" I don't think I've ever heard my father so angry.

But Mom isn't backing down.

"A temperature means that the body is fighting the illness. And I have elderberry syrup to help her get better faster!" She holds up a spoon in one hand and a bottle of thick, dark syrup in the other.

Dad is just staring at her, with an incredulous look on his face.

"That's it," he says. "I'm not listening to your pseudoscience bullshit anymore." With one motion he scoops me out of my bed and carries me out of my room and down the stairs.

"We're going to Urgent Care, and then she'll be at

my house until she's well. I'll call you and let you know what the doctor says."

As we leave the house, I'm glad that I can't see the look on my mom's face. I'm sure she's super-pissed off.

I keep my eyes closed during the short trip to Urgent Care. When I feel the car slow down and ease into the parking lot, I open them a crack. Funny— we're at the same Urgent Care where Dr. Tyrell diagnosed Angie's leukemia. I wonder if he'll be here.

Dad opens my door, and I start climbing out of my seat. He grabs my arm, as if he's afraid I might fall.

"Can you walk? I can carry you, if you want me to."

"No, I can walk. Just let me hold on to you if I need to."

We make our way very slowly to the front door. I'm still clutching the comforter from my bed around my shivering body—Dad grabbed it along with me.

At the check-in desk he tells the woman, "My daughter has a fever of 103.6. She's been feeling bad since yesterday. Can you have a doctor see her right away?"

"I'll get her in as soon as I can," she replies. "We have people ahead of you. Have a seat and fill out these forms." She hands him a clipboard and turns away, dismissing us.

"Wait a minute," I hear through my brain fog. Dad stops and steers us back toward the desk. I try to focus on the person who's speaking, and I'm surprised to see Dr. Tyrell.

"You're the doctor," I croak.

"Yes, I am," he replies. "You can come back now. I'll come around and bring you to the room."

The door from the waiting room into the exam

area opens, and there's Dr. Tyrell, gesturing with his arm for us to enter. As I pass him, we lock eyes.

"I know you," he says to me. I nod my head.

"I came in with my friend Angie," I whispered. "In early October. You diagnosed her leukemia."

"That's right. I remember both of you. You're a good friend. You took good care of her."

He points us to a room marked Number 2.

"Looks like someone needs to take care of you, now. Hop up on the table for me, please."

Dad helps me up on the table. I feel so weak. But something is nagging me in the back of my brain. Why did Dr. Tyrell just take us back to a room? When Angie and I came here, they made sure that we had all of the forms filled out, and we had to wait for quite a while.

As he uses an ear thermometer to take my temperature, I ask him, "Why are you doing this and not a nurse?"

"Well, I thought you might need to be seen immediately. When you were standing at the reception desk, I noticed a slight rash on your neck."

He gently moves my hair away from my neck. My hair, by the way, is a complete and total mess. I haven't even brushed it (or my teeth) since Friday morning. And I think today is Saturday.

"Oh," I hear my dad say. "What is that? It looks like—is it possible—is it measles?"

"That's what I suspect, which is why I wanted to get her out of the waiting room. With fewer people vaccinating their children these days, the risk of infection is greater."

Dad sighs heavily.

"Cassidy wasn't vaccinated," he confesses. "Her mother refused. She had full medical control while

Cassidy was growing up."

"Ah," says Dr. Tyrell. "Well, that explains why she would have been susceptible. I'd like to examine her torso, just to make sure."

I lower my warm comforter. I'm just wearing a long-sleeved t-shirt, so it isn't hard for the doctor to lift it and look at my back.

"Take a look at this," he says, pointing. "She has little red bumps all over her back. Cassidy, can I please look at your stomach?"

I lift the front of my t-shirt and expose my tummy to Dr. Tyrell and my dad.

"It's here, too," says the doctor. "She has the measles."

"Shit," says my dad. "How serious is this?"

"She's a healthy young woman, so she'll probably be fine. Keep an eye on her. We'll treat the symptoms, so give her ibuprofen or acetaminophen for the fever. Keep her hydrated and comfortable. Make extra sure that you watch her breathing. Measles could go to the lungs and cause pneumonia. We don't want that to happen. Keep her away from people who may not be vaccinated, or who are immunocompromised."

"I will." Dad drapes the comforter over my shoulders. It feels good—I'm chilly. "Let's go home, kiddo. We'll swing by CVS on the way."

I don't feel like speaking, so I nod. I feel wiped out. Even though I haven't done anything except sit on the exam table, I am completely exhausted. I lay down on the table while Dad goes back to the lobby to finally fill out the forms and pay for the visit.

When he comes back to get me, I'm fast asleep.

"Come on, Cass, let's go home." He lifts me in his arms and carries me out to the car. I fall asleep again. I don't even notice that he makes a stop at CVS, but I do notice when he gets back in the car.

"I got some good stuff for you. Something to make your throat feel better, ibuprofen for your fever, some oatmeal bath stuff for the itching, and a humidifier, too, so it'll be a little easier to breathe."

"'Kay," I mumble in response. That's all I can get out. But in my head I'm thinking that all sounds pretty dang cool, and a soothing bath when I get to Dad's house might not be a bad idea.

Dad lives in a cute townhouse, not too far from Mom's and my house in Richardson. It's a narrow two story with two bedrooms, two and a half bathrooms, and an office. I don't spend too many nights here, but I have a few things in his guest room that make it mine. A vintage lamp, similar to the one in my room at home, stands on the nightstand. The deep purple comforter is one that I bought at Target just a few months before. And there's a bookshelf packed with my favorites. A small dresser holds some essentials like underwear, shorts, and t-shirts.

The newest addition to the room is a TV mounted to the wall across from the bed. That'll be useful to me later, but right now I just want to take a bath, then hide under the covers.

Dad helps me upstairs, and we both enter my room.

"Here's one of those oatmeal packets," he says, as he hands it to me. "You go take your bath, and I'll get the humidifier set up in here. Don't take too long, honey, okay?"

I nod, grab some clean pajamas from the dresser and make my way to the bathroom. I turn on the tap in the tub until it is about as hot as I can handle. As it's filling, I sprinkle the oatmeal into the water. It really does look like the oatmeal that you cook for breakfast. But I notice that it dissolves once it's mixed in with the water for a bit.

I peel off my grubby clothes and leave them in a pile on the bathroom floor. Sorry, Dad. But there is no way that I'm going to deal with laundry right now. I climb into the tub gingerly—I'm a bit worried that I might slip and fall. I'm still feeling groggy.

The water is bordering on too hot—it feels so wonderful on my freezing skin. I slide all the way down and dunk my head under. It is heaven.

There's a knock on the door, and Dad calls to me, "Cassidy, are you doing okay?"

"Yeah, I'll be out in a couple minutes."

"All right—I'll wait for you in your room."

I rinse off under the shower, so there wouldn't be any residual oatmeal stuck to me, and dress in the clean, soft pajamas. God, they feel so good.

In my room, the humidifier is humming softly and sending cool mist into the air. The blinds are closed, and the bedside lamp glows softly. My comfy bed is calling me.

Dad's there, examining the label of a bottle of something.

"Okay, take two of these for your fever and a spoonful of this for your throat." I do as I'm told. "There's also a water bottle here for you and a cup of hot tea with honey. Are you hungry?"

"No, I just want to sleep," I groan.

"That's what I thought. I'll check on you from time to time, but if you need me just text me."

I nod as I crawl into bed. Dad places my phone on my nightstand, next to the lamp. I notice that he plugs it in for me. He thinks of everything.

I snuggle deeply into my comfy bed and think that I might actually get some decent sleep, when I hear the sound of Dad's voice through my open door. His office is across the hall from my room. It sounds like he stopped there to make a phone call.

"I'd like to speak with one of the nurses caring for Angie Gutiérrez. I have some information that I think is important." There's a pause, then he continues, "Hello, Nicole, my name is Mark Coleman. I'm Cassidy Coleman's father. She's close friends with Angie, and I need to let you know that she was diagnosed with the measles today."

He's quiet for a moment, and I figure he's listening to the nurse at the hospital.

"Sure. If you need anything else from me, please don't hesitate to call." He recites his phone number, then says good-bye.

I spend the next three days sleeping. Dad brings me soup and toast, and I eat a little, but I really don't have much of an appetite. On the fourth day I watch some Netflix—I'm bingeing the new *Lost in Space*. Well, bingeing between naps.

That night, I finally feel well enough to get out of bed and go downstairs. Dad's in the kitchen making a sandwich. It looks really good. I don't realize how hungry I am, until I see those thin slices of roast beef, those juicy tomatoes, and the tangy cheddar cheese.

"Hey, Cass," Dad greets me. "You look better! Want a sandwich?"

"Yeah, that looks really good. But maybe just half of one."

As Dad makes my sandwich, I get a glass of ice water. I look down at my arm, and the rash looks like it's getting better. It isn't as bright and angry looking as it was before.

"There are some of those chips that you like in the pantry," Dad nods in the direction of the open pantry door.

I find the bag of Boulder Canyon chips in the pantry and open it. I love these chips more than life itself. Especially the malt vinegar and sea salt flavor.

Dad and I position ourselves on the two easy chairs in front of the TV and dig into our dinners. I'm able to eat most of the sandwich and all of the chips, which we take as a good sign. I'm recovering.

We watch the latest movie in *The Conjuring* series—it has to do with the Mexican legend of La Llorona. She's the crying woman who takes children who don't behave. The movie doesn't seem to have much in common with the other Conjuring movies, but I still like it. It has some very creepy moments.

That night I sleep soundly and restfully. It feels like I'm finally on my way to recovery, and I'm so relieved.

The next day is Wednesday. I've already missed two days of school, and Dad says I should probably stay home the whole week. We'll see. If I'm fever-free for 24 hours and my rash is gone, then it should be okay for me to go back to school. Dad is still working from home and taking care of me, which is great, but I don't think he really needs to. He says he just wants to make sure I'm all right. Secretly, I'm glad. I like having him around.

I spend quite a bit of the day awake, and we're getting ready to make dinner. Dad is making his famous mac and cheese from scratch. His secret ingredients are bacon and jalapeños. Seriously delicious.

I'm really starting to feel better, which puts me in such a good mood. You don't realize how much you miss doing everyday things. I felt so horrible. My fever was pretty high the whole time, and the rash was really itchy. I think I got lucky that I didn't have any trouble breathing, like Dr. Tyrell said I might. Dad, of course, was awesome the whole time. He takes great care of me.

I'm just thinking that I haven't spoken to Angie in several days. I can't go see her in the hospital, of course, but I haven't even texted or called. I feel bad about that. Honestly, I wasn't thinking of anything besides sleep while I was smack in the middle of this measles garbage.

I pick up my phone from the kitchen counter and send her a text, asking how she's doing. I include a quick explanation of my previous few days, along with a quick apology for not checking in sooner.

The message is delivered, and about a minute later the phone rings. Angie's number is displayed, along with a picture of the two of us.

"Hey, girl! How are things?" I ask as I answer the call.

"Cassidy," comes the reply, "this is Angie's mother."

That's a surprise. Why is Mrs. Gutiérrez answering Angie's phone?

"Oh, hi, Mrs. Gutiérrez. I just wanted to say hi to Angie. I haven't talked to her in a few days."

When Angie's mother speaks next, her voice sounds ragged. Like she isn't getting enough air into her lungs to form the words she needs to say.

"I have to tell you something. I—I don't know how to say this." There's a pause, and it sounds like she's starting to cry. Holy crap, what is happening?

"What's wrong? Can I talk to Angie?" I'm starting to get kind of insistent with her. I feel a very strong need to talk to my friend, right this second.

"Cassidy," Mrs. Gutiérrez is full-blown sobbing now. "Angie died last night. She got the measles and that turned into pneumonia. The infection went through her whole body and she became septic. They took her to the ICU but there was nothing they could do to save her. She's gone."

I am hearing things. My brain must still be fuzzy from my illness, and I'm not understanding what she's saying to me. Or maybe the cell coverage is bad. That happens all the time.

"Mrs. Gutiérrez, you'll need to say that again. I think our connection was messed up."

"Cassidy," she begins, "I know this is hard to take in. You have to listen to me. Angie died last night. She contracted the measles. That turned into pneumonia. That turned into sepsis."

But I'm not listening anymore. I don't hear anything after the words, "Angie died last night." The phone slips from my fingers and I sink to my knees. My breath is shallow—I'm trying to pull air into my lungs, but it isn't working.

I hear Dad somewhere behind me calling my name—he rushes over to me and kneels down in front of me. I know that he's talking, but I can't hear him, much less understand him, through the ringing in my head.

"Slow your breathing, Cass! Breathe in, one, two, three. Now, breathe out, one, two, three."

I do my best to focus on his voice. If I don't, I know that I will probably pass out. One, two, three.

STUCK

"One, two, three," Dad keeps saying, and I keep doing it. Finally, I feel like I'm able to breathe normally.

And I'm hearing Angie's mother's words again.

"Angie died. Measles. Pneumonia. Sepsis."

Measles.

Dad is silently kneeling next to me, his hand resting on my shoulder. I'm still on the floor, bent forward, clutching my stomach. I feel sick—sicker than the measles has made me.

I raise my eyes to look at him. His face is grim. He doesn't know what happened, but he knows it's bad.

"Dad," I whisper hoarsely. "I killed Angie."

Chapter Nineteen

I don't go to school the rest of the week. I don't go back to my mom's house. I don't get out of bed except to use the bathroom. Dad brings me food, but I don't eat anything. I never want to leave my bed again. Honestly, I don't think there's any need to.

From deep within the cocoon of my blankets, I can hear the faint creak of my bedroom door opening. I really don't want any company. Unfortunately, Dad seems to have other plans. I feel him sit down on the bed next to me. He pulls the blankets away from my head. The bright light hurts my eyes, even though they're still closed. Apparently, Dad finds it necessary to open the blinds and let the sunlight in.

"Cass," he says softly. I ignore him.

"Cass," he repeats. He strokes my hair away from my eyes, then he gently shakes my shoulder.

"The funeral's today. You have to go."

At the sound of the word "funeral" I feel like I'll start crying—but no tears come. I think I'm all cried out. It's like there are a finite number of tears in my body, and I used them all because Angie died.

"I don't want to go."

"I know, honey," he sighs. "I know. The hardest things we have to do are usually the most important. You need to be there for Angie's parents."

"I'm still sick," I mumble.

"No, sweetie, you're not. You haven't had a fever for two days, and the rash is completely gone."

"Dad, Angie's parents don't want to see me. They hate me." I'm wrong about the tears—a few of them start to stream down my cheeks.

"Honey, I really don't think that's true. You and Angie were best friends your whole lives. I think her parents would be really disappointed if you didn't come. And I'll be with you the entire time. I won't leave your side."

With aching slowness, I sit up.

"There you go," Dad says, with a slight smile. "We have an hour before we need to leave. That's time for you to shower and have a little something to eat."

He stands up and walks to the door to my room. On the top of the door hangs a hanger containing clothes that I recognize. A pair of black jeans and a navy sweater. Dad reaches up and takes down the hanger.

"I stopped by your mom's and she gave me this outfit for today. She gave me some shoes, too," and he gestures toward the floor.

"Okay," I say. "I'll shower and come downstairs."

As Dad leaves the room, I stand and make my way

into the bathroom. I turn the water on and wait for it to get nice and hot. Then I step in and let the scalding water stream down my head and body. I stand there for several moments, letting the water rinse away the worst of my guilt.

I realize that I haven't given my mother a thought in several days. Not since I learned the terrible news. But then Dad mentioned that Mom gave him the outfit that I'm to wear to Angie's funeral. So, he stopped by and saw her. He talked to her.

I wonder what Mom thinks about this whole horrible situation. My best friend, the friend who I have known since fourth grade, is dead. She had cancer, of course, but it wasn't the cancer that killed her. It was the fact that because her immune system was so wrecked by chemotherapy, her poor body wasn't able to fight off the measles. The measles that I had brought to her hospital bed. We shared a freaking fork!

What does my mother think of this? My mother, who refused to have me vaccinated as a small child, and who believes that vaccines caused Angie's leukemia.

What is she thinking now? I want to find out.

I finish showering and dress quickly in the clothes Dad brought me. In the kitchen, he has a steaming mug of coffee and some scrambled eggs waiting for me. They look and smell better than I thought they would. I must be hungry.

I sit on a simple, wooden bar stool to eat my breakfast. Dad's pouring a cup of java for himself. He's already dressed in a very nice dark suit. He even wears the tie I gave him for Father's Day last year.

"Do you know if Mom will be there?" I ask, as I take a small bite of eggs. He even sprinkled some shredded cheddar on top, which is amazing. I know I need to eat more. The jeans I'm wearing are a bit looser around my waist than I remember.

"Yeah, I'm pretty sure she will be. Do you want to go back to her house with her?"

Actually, I've been considering this very question. After years of living with essential oils and turmeric tea, I'm not sure I want to be around Mom and her ideals right now. I saw the good work that doctors and nurses performed with my own eyes. I don't think her opinions are the right ones anymore.

It's strange to me to feel this complete change of heart. The entire time I lived with Mom, I have never given her non-traditional views much thought. This is just the way she is. Her hippie clothes are trendy, and she makes some delicious vegetarian meals. I never thought anything she did would ever harm anyone. Now, I'm not so sure.

I feel myself shifting some of the blame I've been feeling for days away from myself, and to my mother. In my heart, I know it isn't fair of me to do that. But it definitely makes me feel better. I have a mission now, to confront my mother and grill her until she admits her guilt.

I finish my breakfast and practically run to the car.

Dad parks in the side lot of St. Paul the Apostle Catholic Church. We walk together up the stone steps, toward the huge double doors. The blue sky is tantalizing—the bright sun is blinding. It doesn't seem right, that Angie's funeral is taking place on such a lovely day.

I accompanied Angie and her family to many Sunday services at this beautiful church. As Dad and I enter the nave, I notice the white casket up front, at the sanctuary. Thank goodness it's closed. I wouldn't have been able to hold myself together if it had been open.

Dad and I find a couple of seats toward the back.

I scan the crowd to see who I recognize. It looks like our entire high school class is in attendance. The place is packed. As I look around, I notice Miranda walking up the aisle. She looks lovely, in a burgundy-colored, knee-length dress. She definitely stands out in the sea of black.

We make eye contact, and she makes her way over to me. I rise to meet her. I'm not sure how she'll react to me, and I'm nervous. I'm half expecting her to haul off and hit me. Angie's death is, after all, my fault.

Instead, she wraps her arms around me for several long moments. When she lets go and steps back she asks, "Are you okay?"

I consider lying to her and saying, "Sure, yes, of course!" But I realize that Miranda has become a close friend, and she doesn't deserve that.

"No," I admit. "Not really."

She takes my hand, and we both make our way back to where Dad is sitting. We have to ask a few people to scoot over, but we manage to make a spot for Miranda. I sit between her and Dad.

Since we're all sitting in a Catholic church, I'm prepared for the strains of Ave Maria to fill the grand space. Instead, it's Cyndi Lauper's voice singing *True Colors* that begins the service. I tried so hard to be strong. I thought I had prepared myself. But not for this. We had danced together to Cyndi Lauper so many times.

I can't hold it in—I lose it. Shit! I'm digging through my pockets, looking desperately for a tissue, but there's nothing. I'm a total mess—tears and snot are all over my face. Thank God I didn't put on any make-up.

Magically, a handful of tissues appears in front of me. Miranda, to the rescue.

I need that wad of Kleenex to get me through the songs, the speeches, and the slide show. There's even a photo of me—I remember when it was taken. Angie had just won a race, of course, and I'm right behind her. We are hugging. I lose it again.

Coach Johnson delivers the eulogy. He says amazing things about my amazing friend and not just about running. There's the story about how she lost a race once, because she helped a competitor who had tripped over her own dumb shoelaces. The coach speaks about her character and her sportsmanship, and how he had always known that she would have an incredible, bright future ahead of her. He knows that many people will miss her. There isn't a dry eye in the house.

Finally, it's over. Everyone stands as the pall bearers carry Angie's casket up the aisle, toward the open doors. I've had enough. There is no way I can be at the graveside to watch Angie lowered into the ground.

I turn to look at Dad. "Can we go home?"

"Sure, honey. No problem."

"Miranda, do you need a ride?" She's still clutching my hand, looking through the open doors.

She turns to face me. "No, I have my car." Her cheeks are streaked with tear stains. "Will you be at school on Monday?"

"Um…" I begin—then Dad takes over.

"Yes, she definitely will be."

"Okay, good. Maybe…maybe we can hangout this

weekend, if you want to."

"I'm not sure about that, Miranda," my dad interrupts. "That means that Cassidy would actually have to get out of bed and take a shower."

I feel my lips curve into a tiny smile. It's completely involuntary.

"I think I'm out of bed for good, now," I say.

Miranda lets go of my hand, gives me a quick hug, and tells me, "I'll text you later."

The three of us follow the remaining mourners out of the church. The sun shone as brightly as it has earlier, which still seems so wrong to me. I raise my hand to shield the glare of the sun, and when I do, I notice a figure a little bit in front of me with long hair and a flowing dark skirt. It's Mom. She's standing with her back to me.

Finally! I'll have the chance to ask her how she feels about this whole mess that *she* caused.

"Mom!" I call to her.

She turns, and her face lights up when she sees me. A huge smile is on her face as she calls to me and begins walking in my direction.

"Cassidy, sweetie, I missed you!"

Mom pulls me into her arms and squeezes me so tight that I can't breathe. I wriggle out of her grip.

"Mom, wait, I need to talk to you."

"Oh, okay, honey." She brushes my hair across my forehead. "Are you feeling better? You look better. Are you coming home soon?"

"Mom, listen to me!" I have to raise my voice to get her to hear me. She stops, startled. She isn't used to hearing me talk like that.

"What? What is it?"

"I want to know how you feel about everything

that's happened. What do you have to say for yourself?"

A puzzled expression crosses Mom's face.

"What, honey? What do I have to say about what?"

"Angie is dead because of you."

"What?" she gasps. "How can you say that?"

"I caught the measles and gave them to Angie, because you never had me vaccinated. If I'd been vaccinated when I was little, then this never would have happened."

"Now, honey," she begins, as she strokes my arm. "Calm down. You're overreacting. Remember I told you that it was the vaccine that gave Angie leukemia. None of this is your fault, or mine."

I am in shock! Mom's denying all responsibility for what happened to Angie. I can't believe it. In my mind, she and I are equally responsible. I got sick because of her stance on vaccines, and I stupidly visited Angie when I knew I wasn't feeling one-hundred percent. Well, I want to know what she's thinking and I guess now I do.

"You were in the same kitchen for Thanksgiving dinner as me. Didn't you hear what everyone was saying? Especially that nurse. Vaccines work, Mom, and they're not dangerous. They don't cause all of the things you say they do."

"Oh, honey." She's standing in front of me, shaking her head. "I held my tongue during dinner because I didn't want a fight at Thanksgiving. But I think those people are delusional. And I think that nurse was a liar."

I am speechless. How can she not see the truth? My mother is so entrenched in her conspiracy theories, there's no way she'll ever accept any responsibility for what happened to Angie. And here I am, wracked with the guilt of it all.

Shouldn't a mother try to relieve her child of a burden? Maybe even if she doesn't believe it completely, shouldn't she show a little compassion?

I can't talk to her. I can't look at her. I turn to leave.

"Dad," I call. "I'm ready, let's go."

"Cassidy—you need to come home with me!" Mom is behind me, getting a little loud. "The Divorce Decree says you have to!" The pitch of her voice is rising.

I ignore her. I'm going to Dad's.

"Cassidy, you have to come with me!" She's screaming now, running after me and grabbing my arm. People are staring. Apparently, Mom doesn't care. I don't care, either.

I pull free from her grasp.

"No, I don't! I'm not coming with you! I'm staying with Dad. We'll get a lawyer to change the decree. I can't stand you! Angie is dead because of you, and you won't even admit it! I can't believe it! You just need to leave me alone."

When I stop shouting, there is complete silence. No one around us is speaking—they are just staring. Mom and I are piercing each other with our eyes. She is breathing rapidly, like she just ran a 5K. It looks like she is gearing up to start yelling at me again, but before she can I hear a sound behind me.

"Cassidy," Dad says softly. I turn to look at him. "Let's go. Come on, honey."

"Cassidy," Mom shouts. "Come with me. Please."

I feel like I'm the rope caught in the middle of a brutal tug-of-war. Everything I lived with up to Angie's death has changed. I always thought my mother was so cute with her hippie philosophies—her crystals, essential oils, and homeopathic remedies. I never thought any of that can be harmful—certainly not dangerous. Now, seemingly overnight, my opinion has completely changed.

I've always known that she loves me. There was never any question about that. My whole life, she thought she was doing what's best for me. She's simply misinformed.

"Mom, I'll come with you on one condition."

"Okay," she says, a bit skeptically. "What is it?"

"I need you to take me to the doctor and have me vaccinated for everything I've missed so far."

"No. I will never agree to that. Because I love you. I will never agree to put poison in your body."

I look at Dad, and then back at Mom. I know what I have to do.

"Bye, Mom. I'll see you."

As Dad and I begin walking toward the car, I hear her behind me, still screeching my name.

Chapter Twenty

When we're back at Dad's we both end up in the kitchen. He grabs a bottle of Shiner from the fridge, and I grab a Dr. Pepper, in honor of Angie.

There's a comfortable silence between us, like always. We both know that we need to have a conversation about what the future might look like.

I figure I might as well be the one to start. I hop up on one of the stools, and make myself comfortable.

"I really do want to live with you," I begin.

Dad sets his Shiner on the counter and smiles.

"That isn't anything that we need to decide right now. I know things got pretty emotional between you and your mom. We can wait before we make any serious decisions."

"Well, let's say that you and I do decide that I'm gonna live with you. Is that easy to do?" I don't know if we'll have to get lawyers involved, or if I can just say that I want to move in with Dad.

He considers his answer before he speaks.

"The best thing, of course, is if all three of us agree to a move. But if we have to, we can take it to a judge. I don't think we'd need to hire a lawyer, but we could do that. It shouldn't be a big deal. I think that by the time a child reaches your age, a judge would listen to what you want and take it seriously."

This is good news. I have no idea how the legal system works, especially when it comes to divorce and custody. The only information about law and courtrooms I have is from watching *The Good Wife*.

"Does that mean that you can take me to the doctor and get me vaccinated?" I'm pretty hopeful that this can work. If I can say I want to live with my dad, then I can just go to Urgent Care, and say that I want vaccines, right?

"Well, we might be able to get that written into some new court orders, but we can't do anything until that happens."

"But Dad," I begin, "I need to be vaccinated now. Like, I want to get in my car, go to Urgent Care, and get the shots. Today. Angie died because I got the measles and I gave them to her." Emotions are a funny thing. You never know when they're going to come out of nowhere and knock you sideways. "I didn't even get to say good-bye to her! I didn't know what was going on, because I was so sick!"

Tears are welling up in my eyes again—they spill onto my cheeks.

I realize that I'm still processing everything that happened. I didn't speak to Angie's parents at the funeral. Part of me is terrified that they blame me, and they'll hate me forever. But the other part really wants to see them. They are like my other family.

"Oh, sweetie," Dad reaches across the counter and takes my hand. "I know how bad you feel. And I know that I can tell you all day long that this wasn't your fault. I don't want you to blame yourself, but I think it'll just take some time for you to heal."

"You'll let me stay here until we figure things out with the judge, right?" I ask and grip his hand tightly. I still love my mother—it isn't like I never want to see her again. Just not right now. It feels like at the moment we are so divided in our thinking, there's no way we can even be in the same room.

"Of course, Cassidy. You can absolutely stay with me."

"Okay, good." I grab a tissue from the box on the island, wipe my face, and blow my nose. "And you'll take me to get vaccines?"

Dad pulls his phone out of his pocket and begins tapping.

"Honestly, I'm not exactly sure how that works in Texas. I don't think they'd let you go in by yourself, until your eighteen. And I'm still not allowed to make that decision for you. Your mom has complete control over medical decisions, remember?"

"But you could just take me in!" I protest. "We don't have to tell anyone about the divorce paperwork and what is says. You're my dad, and if you say it's okay, then it is!"

This makes total sense to me.

"I really don't feel comfortable doing that, honey. I can get in a lot of trouble by going against those orders. Your mom would not be happy—I know she'd make it hard on me."

He comes around the other side of the island and takes me in his arms. This is my safe place. I'll never be too big for a daddy hug.

"Honey, I know that you feel the need to do all of this right now. I do. But it's not going to happen right away. We need to follow the process, and that'll take time. You're going to have to wait a while. But I promise that on Monday, I'll start looking into getting those orders changed."

He releases his hold on me and lifts my chin to look in my eyes.

"Okay?"

There is nothing I can do but agree with him.

"Okay," I reply. But today is Saturday, and Monday seems far off.

"I think I'm going to drive around for a bit," I say. I reach for my Dr. Pepper, and my car keys. "I might swing by Angie's house. I haven't talked to her parents. I think I probably should."

"Sounds good." Dad loosens his tie and makes his way upstairs to change clothes. "I'll be here – I'm not planning to go anywhere. Call me if you need anything."

I hop into Elsa and back out of the driveway. Angie's house is just a few blocks away from Dad's, which is also just a few blocks away from Mom's. When Mom bought the house many years earlier, Dad decided to move into the same neighborhood, so he'd be close to me. That didn't mean much to me when I was younger, but now I understand how incredibly cool that was.

I know a lot of kids whose parents are divorced, but most of them don't live as close to each other as mine do. Even though I officially live with my mother,

I always know that I can walk to Dad's any time I need or want to.

And, since we all live within the same school district, Angie's house is pretty much right around the corner. Or, I suppose now I should refer to it as "Angie's Parents' House."

As I pull onto Angie's street (I suppose it'll always be her street) I notice a ton of cars parked along both sides. As I get closer to the house, I realize they all seem to be visiting Mr. and Mrs. Gutiérrez. It hasn't occurred to me that there would be a get-together after the funeral. But now I remember—it's common for the mourners to assemble at the family's home.

I have to park pretty far from the house because of all the cars. As I make my way along the sidewalk, I am again struck by how beautiful the day is. The sky is so blue, and the temperature is warm for early December. It's the kind of day that Angie and I would have spent on the Bluebonnet Trail, riding our bikes or going for a long, slow jog that would last for hours.

I walk up the steps of the house—the screen door is closed, but the heavy, wooden door is wide open. There are dozens of people inside, so I just open the screen door and let myself in.

In the dining room the large table is heavy with so many different dishes. I see platters of tamales and enchiladas and also lasagna and green salads. People are in every room, eating and speaking in Spanish. I catch a few words here and there—Angie's parents have tried to teach me over the years.

I'm not quite sure what to do. I feel out of place because I'm not with anyone and no one expects me. Then, I feel a hand on my shoulder. I turn and look into Angie's father's eyes.

They are impossible to read. I try to discern his thoughts and his feelings—is he furious with me? Does he hate me? I wouldn't blame him one little bit if he did. But then I notice his eyes soften, and he reaches out his arms to me. I fall into him and begin sobbing. Just when I think I'm all cried out...

Mr. Gutiérrez isn't a tall man—we are just about the same height, and my head is able to rest comfortably on his shoulder. He pats my back and whispers, "Shhhh…" until I finally calm down.

I'm still hiccupping as I step back and whisper, "I'm sorry." That's when I notice that Angie's mom has appeared next to her husband. She's smiling softly and shaking her head at me.

"Sweetheart, there's no need for you to be sorry. You did nothing wrong. Angie was very sick. It wasn't anyone's fault," she assures me.

I'm shaking my head, my eyes shut tight. I don't believe one word.

"But we were sitting so close to each other on Thanksgiving and eating the same piece of pie. I was getting my germs all over her." And, here come the sobs again.

Mrs. Gutiérrez grabs a bottle of water from the fridge and twists the cap off. She takes my hand and then leads me out the back door to the patio. We sit next to each other on the comfy outdoor couch.

In the summer there are vegetable beds filled to the brim with tomatoes, tomatillos, cucumbers, and lettuce. Now, most of the beds have been cleaned and winterized, but some of the herbs and lettuce are still going strong.

Angie and her mom had always loved gardening together. Angie was always so excited when spring was on the horizon. When the days started getting longer, she knew it was time for her and her mom to prepare the beds. Then in mid to late March, they spent an entire weekend planting all kinds of seedlings.

Now, Angie's mom will do this alone.

"The herbs and lettuce are still looking good," I say, pointing toward the garden.

"Yes, they are," Mrs. Gutiérrez replies. "If you like, you can help me plant in the spring."

I nod, not really sure if I want to do that. I would feel like I was taking Angie's place.

She takes my hand in hers. I gaze at her hand clasping mine. I'm not able to look in her eyes.

"Cassidy, sweetheart, I don't want you to spend one more minute blaming yourself. The last thing I want is for you to feel guilty. Angie had cancer. That's what killed her."

She cups my chin gently and raises my head.

"I mean it," she says. Now we are gazing directly in each other's eyes. "You look into my eyes, and you know I'm not lying. I love you, Cassidy. You are like a daughter to me. We will get through this together."

She sounds really sincere. It's hard for me to believe that she can still love me and not hate me forever. But I'm glad she does.

We hug for a long moment and I drink a little more from the water bottle. Then we just sit on the couch, looking out into the garden.

"Do you remember the pumpkin patch?" I ask her.

"Oh, yes," she replies. A smile spreads across her face. "That was fun, wasn't it? You girls had so much fun picking out the perfect one. You know, I'm always surprised how many pumpkins can grow on just a single vine."

"I loved that," I say. "Maybe we can plant some pumpkins in the spring."

She turns to look at me and squeezes. "Yes. We'll definitely do that."

Mrs. Gutiérrez begins offering me something to eat, but I'm not really hungry.

"Let me put some salsa verde in a container for you to take home," she insists.

I'm not going to say no to that—her salsa verde is the best in the world.

"How many habaneros did you add?" The more, the better, in my opinion.

"Plenty!" she replies. "My family likes it hot and spicy just like you do."

We go back in the house together, Mrs. Gutiérrez's hand resting on my shoulder. In the kitchen I grab a plastic container from the cabinet that I've rummaged through thousands of times before. Mrs. Gutiérrez is holding the big bowl of salsa—she ladles a good amount into my plastic container. I'm set with salsa for at least a week.

She snaps the lid on tight and hands it to me. Our fingers touch as I take the plasticware from her.

"I'll head home now," I say, a little hesitantly. This house has been my second home for years. I want to stay, but I know it's time to go.

"Goodbye, sweetheart," she wraps her arms around me and kisses my cheek. "Come back soon, okay?"

I assure her that I will, and I go out the front door and down the block where I parked Elsa. I drive through the neighborhood without a destination in mind. The sights bring back so many memories. There's the park where Angie and I had played when we were little. It's part of the wooded greenbelt where all kinds of wildlife lived. When we walked or jogged along the path at dusk, we often saw coyotes.

I park the car by the bridge and get out. The bridge crossed "our" creek (of course we thought everything was ours when we were little girls) and it connects two separate neighborhoods. I stand in the middle of the bridge and gaze down into the water. There's been quite a bit of rain during the past few weeks, so the water is higher than it has been in a while. It's rushing by quickly; I remember how Angie would call it a "raging river" when we watched it together.

The sound of children's voices is all around me. It's a perfect day to be out riding on a bike, or playing among the trees. Birds sing and the water below me gurgles and bubbles. I hate that the day is so pretty and Angie is in the ground.

Just like that, I know where I need to go next. You know in cartoons, when you see a light bulb over someone's head because they just got a bright idea? It is just like that.

I jog back to Elsa, climb in, and turn the key. I have a mission now. A purpose. I'm going to Urgent Care to see Dr. Tyrell.

Chapter Twenty-One

I pull into the parking lot and am pleased to see that there are hardly any cars there. On the drive over, I was thinking about how I'd get to see Dr. Tyrell. I'm not sick, and they probably aren't going to just let me chat with him. I don't even know if he'll be there. But, if he is, I'll go in and say that I'm there for a follow-up visit for my measles. I want to make sure that everything is okay, and that I'm well.

So, at the reception desk, that's what I tell them. And I get their attention.

"Measles?" the receptionist asks, an incredulous expression on her face. "You had the measles?"

"Right, and I just want to follow up with Dr. Tyrell to make sure everything is okay now. He told me I should come back when my fever and the rash were gone." That may have been a little fib. I don't think he told Dad that I need to come back. But I don't think this gal would know that.

"Uh, okay," she says, as she gets up from her chair. "Just stay right there, and I'll be right back."

Once again, I don't need to sit in the waiting area with the other patients. They take this measles thing pretty seriously. Within just a few minutes Dr. Tyrell opens the door and motions me to follow him back to the exam area.

I follow him into a room, and he closes the door behind us. I hop up onto the table.

"What's up, Cassidy?" he asks. "You look a lot better. Are you still not feeling well?"

"No, I'm much better. But I need you to vaccinate me against any other diseases I might get."

"Oh!" Dr. Tyrell sounds surprised. "Okay…How old are you, Cassidy?"

"I'm 16. I'll be 17 in a few months."

"Cassidy, I'm sorry. I can't vaccinate you without a parent's consent. Didn't your dad bring you in when you were sick?"

"Yeah, he did," I reply. I don't like where this is going.

"Have him come in with you, and he can sign the consent form."

"I don't think that'll work. He told me that the divorce paperwork states that my mom makes all medical decisions. He's going to call a lawyer and try to get that changed. But that'll take time, and I don't want to wait."

"Can't you come in with your mom? Won't she sign the paperwork?" It makes perfect sense to Dr. Tyrell. I wish it were that easy.

"No. She thinks vaccines are poison."

"Oh…I see," he's nodding slowly. He doesn't need

to say a word—I know what he's thinking by the look in his eyes. The conversation from Thanksgiving dinner comes back to me, especially the many points made by the nurse.

"That's too bad. But I'm afraid that it's against the law for me to vaccinate you without a parent's consent."

It occurs to me that the doctor probably doesn't know what happened to Angie. Why would he? No one from the hospital would have told him.

"Did you hear what happened to Angie?" I ask.

"Your friend with leukemia? No, what happened?"

"I gave her my measles, and she died." I figure the direct approach would be the best.

"What? I thought she was at Children's getting treatment!" Dr. Tyrell exclaims. His eyes widen in surprise.

"She was," I reply. "Chemo didn't work, and then they were going to do something called CAR T. While she was waiting for that to happen, I got the measles. I was just starting to get a cough and I didn't think anything of it." My eyes are filling with tears again. "I went to the hospital after our Thanksgiving dinner, so she could have some turkey and pie."

The memory of that night comes flooding back to me. The two of us sitting so close together, sharing a piece of pie. And the concierge downstairs, asking me if I was feeling okay. Why the hell hadn't I told them that I was getting a cough? If I had done that, they probably would have sent me away. I would have been pissed off, and I'm sure I would have argued with them, but Angie would still be alive.

"I didn't know it was the measles!" I'm full-blown sobbing now. Snot is mixing with tears again and I'm a total wreck. Dr. Tyrell grabs the box of tissues from the computer table and hands me the whole thing. It helps a bit.

"I didn't know that anyone could die from the measles," I whimper, beginning to calm down a little.

I blow my nose and wipe my face, then throw the sopping tissues in the trash can. Dr. Tyrell has his back to me, and, when he turns around, he hands me a small plastic cup filled with water. The top of the cup has ridges, like a lid could be screwed on top of it. I raise an eyebrow.

"Is this a cup that someone pees into?" I ask. This seems suspicious.

He chuckles. "Yes, but don't worry, it's never been used for that. So, regarding the measles, most of the time people recover from an illness like that. It's only if they're very old, very young, or if there's a problem with the patient's immune system that it's potentially fatal."

Like Angie—her immune system was non-existent because of all the chemo.

"What other diseases do you vaccinate for?" I need to know how else I could possibly harm the population of my hometown.

"Well, there's chicken pox," he begins.

"I already had those. Can I get them again?" I interrupt.

"It isn't likely. But, it's not a bad idea to give you the vaccine, just to make sure. It can't hurt anything. Same thing with the measles."

"Okay, what else?"

"Mumps, rubella, hepatitis, polio, tetanus, whooping cough, and meningitis." He closes his eyes for a moment. "HPV, also—there are probably a few more that I'd need to double-check. We'd do that before we administered anything to you, of course."

"Okay," I say and take another sip of water. "Which diseases are the most dangerous?"

"There isn't really an easy answer to that, Cassidy. Say you step on a rusty nail—you could get tetanus, which is a danger to you. But that can't be transmitted to another person easily. Now, whooping cough, on the other hand, is contagious and again it can be very dangerous to some people."

"I really need you to give me those vaccines" I'm trying to be as forceful as possible, without sounding downright rude. "I can't do this to another person. Please!" I'm begging now, but I don't care. I need to convince him somehow.

"I wish I could—I really do. But it's absolutely illegal for me to do that without consent from a parent."

"But that doesn't make sense!" I argue. "I've been here plenty of times to get a sports physical so I could run track. And that was by myself! I never came here with my mom or dad. I would tell them that I needed a physical, and they told me to come here to get it done. Nobody ever had a problem with it!"

Dr. Tyrell thinks for a moment before he answers. He bends over his laptop, apparently checking something in the medical system.

"Ah, I thought so. We have a consent form from your mother on file. But it specifies that you can only come in by yourself and receive a simple sports physical. Anything more than that, and we would need her consent," he explains. "That's the difference."

"Well I don't see a difference! All I know is that I killed my best friend and I absolutely cannot risk doing something like that again! What if, I somehow come down with whooping cough and my 75-year-old grandma comes for a visit? Just like with Angie, I don't know I'm sick. Or, I don't realize how serious it is. And I end up killing her, just like I did Angie!"

I can tell that Dr. Tyrell feels sorry for me and my situation, but I haven't quite convinced him yet.

"Do you realize that I will have to live with this for the rest of my life? This knowledge that my best friend in the whole world died because of me. It wasn't leukemia that killed her—it was me. The worst thing is that when I think about it, I realize that the whole thing could have been prevented. It didn't have to happen this way. If only I had gotten those shots when I was little, then Angie would be alive today. I know there was no guarantee that the cancer wouldn't have gotten her. I get it. But at least she would have had a fighting chance! How am I supposed to live with this?"

He doesn't say anything—he's listening, which is what I want.

"At least, if you agree to vaccinate me, I will feel confident that I've done everything possible to keep something terrible like this from happening again. And, I promise you, I won't tell a soul. Never. I don't need this for school records. I'm already in school. I need this for me. I need this to make sure that I don't hurt anyone in this way ever again. Please."

I'm sitting on the exam table, waiting for his reply. My eyes are no longer streaming, but I know they are terribly red and puffy. He leans against the sink across from me. His arms are folded across his chest. I can tell he is thinking, and I don't want to say anything. I've said what I need to say.

I hold my breath. There is no sound in the small

room—I hear some faint laughter from far away, but that's it.

He looks at me and speaks very softly.

"Okay. I'll do it."

I don't say anything—I don't want to destroy the moment and possibly change his mind.

Then he says it again.

"I'll do it, Cassidy. I'll vaccinate you. We'll start today with Measles- Mumps- Rubella and Diphtheria-Pertussis- Tetanus. You'll need a second round of both in two months. The schedule for adults or, 'almost adults' like you, is a little different than for small children."

He pauses and gazes at me intently.

"You're sure, Cassidy?"

I nod. "Yes, I'm absolutely sure. I don't want to take these chances again. I don't want to hurt anyone else."

"All right. I'll be back in a minute." Dr. Tyrell opens the door and leaves the examination room.

While I wait for him to come back, I think about my mother. I know she'll be furious with me if she ever finds out about this. Although I'm not too thrilled with her at the moment, I truly hope we'll be okay—sooner rather than later. I still love my mom. I can't imagine not having her in my life. And even if I do decide to move in with my dad, which I still might, there's no reason for me to stay mad at my mom forever. I'll have to figure out the best way to make up with her. Without her finding out about the vaccines, of course. That's between me and Dr. Tyrell.

I'll touch base with her sometime during the week, once we've both had some time to cool off.

The door opens and Dr. Tyrell reenters the room.

He's carrying a metal tray with two syringes. Okay then—this is getting real.

"Roll up a sleeve, Cassidy. We'll do one in each arm."

Luckily, I'm wearing a t-shirt so it isn't hard to roll up my sleeves. I feel excited and nervous, at the same time. It's like I'm doing something really rebellious, which is silly. I'm not out getting a tattoo—just vaccines, which most people get when they're very young.

The doctor swabs my upper arm with some rubbing alcohol.

"Here we go!" he announces.

Then I feel a small pinch and that's it. The second shot is the same.

"All done! Come back in two months for the second round." He begins typing on the laptop sitting on the counter. "I'll enter this information into your records." Dr. Tyrell turns to face me and says, a little sternly, "It's your responsibility to come back when it's time for the next set of vaccines. No one will call you to set it up."

"Yes, of course, I'll put it in my phone."

"Good. Most people don't have any type of reaction to the vaccine. Your arm might be a little sore, and you might run a slight fever. You might even feel a little run-down tomorrow, but all of those reactions are completely normal. If you feel anything more serious, let me know. Okay?"

I nod. "Sure. And, I promise, I won't tell anyone."

Dr. Tyrell smiles at me. "Thanks, Cassidy. I appreciate that."

Chapter Twenty-Two

Monday is going to be my first day back at school since I got sick, and since Angie died. I feel torn about going back. It isn't right that I'll be able to go to school, see all of my friends, and run track, when Angie is lying in the cemetery. But I long to have the normalcy of my regular life back. I'm looking forward to going back to school.

Sunday evening is spent getting ready for the week. I know I have missed a lot of schoolwork—it will take some time to get caught up. But that's okay. I have time.

Dr. Tyrell was right—I don't have any negative reaction to the vaccines. All day Sunday I feel fine. Dad and I go shopping at Costco and he grills steaks for us that evening. Other than that, it's a boring Sunday. That's just fine with me.

My dad's the absolute best steak griller in Texas. There's no need to go to a steak house, ever. He has one of those big, egg-shaped ceramic grills, and he'll throw in a handful of wood chips on top of the coals for a smoky flavor. I make some roasted potatoes and a cucumber salad to go along with the steaks.

We're washing the dishes together when suddenly we hear loud banging on the front door. We look at each other and ask at the same time, "Are you expecting someone?" I guess that answers both of our questions.

The pounding continues and then we hear a voice that joins it. Our attention is now riveted on the door and the noise coming from beyond it.

"Cassidy! I know you're in there! Open this door!"

I recognize my mother's voice.

"Oh crap," I say, as I meet my father's eyes. "She sounds pissed."

"She sure does," Dad replies, as he walks toward the door. "Any idea why?"

"Uh, no, I don't think so." There's no way she could have found out what I did. It's impossible.

She keeps pounding on the door—it sounds like it's going to break off its hinges. I never thought my mild-mannered mom could make such a racket

Dad opens the door and lets her in.

"Beth, what's wrong?" he asks her, but he doesn't get an answer. My tiny mother storms past him, her long skirt swirling around her legs, her hair flowing. She stops in front of me and grabs my arm, pushing up the sleeve of my t-shirt. A Band-Aid that is still on my upper arm is exposed for all of us to see.

Still clutching my arm tightly, Mom drags me to where my dad stands. She's really squeezing and it hurts. I try to pull away, but she holds tight.

"Mark, what the hell is this? What have you done?"

Dad, of course, looks perplexed. He has no idea what she is talking about.

"Beth, what is that?"

"Oh, don't you play dumb with me! You took Cassidy to the doctor and had her vaccinated! You know you're not supposed to do that—*I* make all of her medical decisions. How dare you?"

Dad holds his hands up defensively. He has a stunned look on his face, and he's shaking his head.

"No, I wouldn't do that. I've always followed the court orders. You know that. Even though you and I disagree, I wouldn't go against the orders." He nods in my direction. "Cassidy and I discussed it, and I explained it to her."

Realization starts to dawn in my mother's eyes. She turns to face me.

"You?" she asks, incredulously. "Did you do this?"

"How—how did you find out?" I stutter. That seems to be the most important question I can think of.

"I have a myChart account and it has all of your medical information. I get e-mail notifications every time it's updated. So every time you went to Urgent Care for a physical, I'd get an e-mail. I happened to get an e-mail yesterday, but I didn't log in until just a little while ago. And it showed me that a Dr. Tyrell vaccinated you."

Ohhhhhh…that's how she found out.

"I talked him into it," I say quietly. "He didn't want to, but I convinced him."

"He's not allowed to do that!" she screeches. "He can't do that without my consent!"

She finally lets go of my arm—I rub it where she was clutching me. Mom breathes in deeply and closes her eyes. I've seen her do this many times. It's her way of calming herself.

"Okay," she sighs, then she turns to look at me. "Cass, I'm not happy with you. You've had poison injected into you, and it's very dangerous."

"Mom, that's not true," I begin, but she holds up her hand to stop me from saying another word.

"Hopefully, there's a way to detox you, but I don't know."

"I don't think I need a detox," I say.

"Well, if I can't find anything, I'll at least bring you some turmeric tea."

She wraps her arms around me and holds me close. I breathe in her familiar fragrance, and I realize that I miss her so much. I hug her back, tightly.

"Do you want to come home with me, sweetie?" she whispers in my ear.

Honestly, part of me does. I miss our old routines and I really miss her cooking. But for the first time in my life I have a chunk of alone time with my dad, and I'm not ready to give that up yet.

I pull out of her embrace and say, "I don't think so, Mom. I'm having a pretty good time here with Dad. But I love you lots, okay? Let me get back into the swing of going to school, and then I'll come see you."

She nods, then walks through the front door without saying good-bye. I look at Dad, knowing I'm in trouble. He folds his arms across his chest. Uh oh.

"What were you thinking? I told you that we would take care of it the right way. I already have an attorney picked out that I'm planning to call on Monday."

"I know, Dad, I'm sorry." I really am, too. But I

also feel very strongly about being vaccinated and not putting other people in danger.

"Dad, I felt so powerless," I explain to him. "There was actually something I could do that would help protect me and other people, and I wasn't allowed to do it. That made no sense to me. And it wasn't like I was out drinking or smoking weed."

That makes him chuckle a little. I'm making progress!

"Most people get these shots when they're really little—before they even start school. You know that, Dad."

"Honey, I agree with you," Dad says, as he walks back to the kitchen. "Come on, let's finish up here." He throws a kitchen towel at my head.

"I absolutely agree with you, kiddo. But we have to go about this the right way. I'm afraid that you might have caused some problems, going about it the way you did."

That gets my attention.

"Problems? What kind of problems?"

"I don't know, but we'll find out."

Elsa and I pick Miranda up on the way to school the next day. I fill her in as I drive.

"Seriously?" she sounds really surprised. "I've never given vaccines any thought—they were just shots I got every now and then when I was a kid."

"I know, right?"

We're about to pass by the Urgent Care where Dr. Tyrell works, and I'm going to point it out to Miranda when the sight in front of me makes me slam on the brakes.

"Holy crap!" exclaims Miranda. "What's your

problem?"

I turn to look at her, and I burst out laughing. A fuchsia line is slashed across her mouth. She is holding lipstick in her right hand.

"I love that shade!"

"Okay, dork, why did you slam on the brakes?"

"Look over there." I nod to the other side of the street from where we're parked. "That's the Urgent Care where Angie was diagnosed with leukemia and where the doctor vaccinated me. Now look what's happening."

In the parking lot of the Urgent Care building, right in front of the automatic double doors, about a dozen people are marching and holding signs that read, "Our Children—Our Choice," and "Freedom Keepers." They're chanting, "Don't poison our kids!" over and over.

The loudest voice of all comes from a tiny woman wearing a long skirt with a long, dark braid hanging down her back. Mom doesn't often tie her hair back—it looks like she's serious.

Miranda and I watch a car pull into the parking lot. A woman and a boy, who looks to be about eight, get out of the car and start to make their way to the front door. The woman puts her hand on the boy's shoulder, and they both hesitate in front of the mob. Okay, maybe it isn't a mob—but they don't want to let the mom and kid through those sliding doors.

I'm watching the mom's face, and her expression becomes one of staunch resolve—she will get through there, no matter what. I can't tell what's wrong with the boy, but he doesn't look too bad off. But I don't think it matters what's wrong with him—his mother is determined to get him in there.

But every time they move toward the doors, the protestors block their path. I would have been very annoyed, if I were them.

It's like they're dancing—no one actually puts their hands on anyone else, but the protestors surge forward and block the pair. They try to go around the mob, but are again blocked. This goes on for a good five minutes, until the mom finally gives up and steers her kid back to the car. Truly, there's another Urgent Care center catty-corner from this one. They're like a dime-a-dozen in Richardson.

Once they left, my mom and her posse take up the chant again. All I hear is, "Our children—our choice."

I see someone from inside the building who's dressed in scrubs come to the front door and assess the situation. I can't tell if it is a nurse or maybe one of the women at the desk. The doors slide open in front of her.

"Excuse me!" I hear her say, trying hard to raise her voice over the chanting. "Excuse me! You have to leave! You can't be here!"

Everyone totally ignores her. They just keep chanting and walking around in that circle in front of the entrance. The poor woman tries yelling at the group a few more times, but it's useless. She turns around and goes back inside.

As soon as she does, a van pulls into the parking lot. It has a big letters and numbers painted on the side—WRIC 11. There's an antenna mounted to the top and also what appears to be a small satellite dish. Oh crap. It's a news van—the media is here.

When they come to a stop, Mom steps out of the line and approaches the passenger side of the van. A well-dressed woman with long blonde hair exits the van and holds her hand out to my mom.

"Hi there!" she says. "I'm Cynthia Mitchell from Channel 11 News. Are you Beth?"

"Yes, that's me," replies Mom. "I'm the one who called you about this deplorable situation. This is where the doctor is, who is vaccinating children without parental consent. It's completely illegal!"

Together they walk toward the protestors. I'm riveted by all of this activity, and I completely forgot that Miranda is sitting in the passenger seat. I turn to face her.

"We should get to school, shouldn't we?" I ask her.

"Oh, hell, no! There's nothing at school that's as interesting as this is."

I grin. "Cool—I don't want to go, either. We can be a little late." Then I have a thought, that I'm not so crazy about. "But let's lay low—the last thing I want is to be on the news." We both scrunch down a little lower in our seats.

A cameraman follows Cynthia and my mom to the group of protestors. Mom holds up a hand, and they all pause their chanting. Then Cynthia speaks.

"Good morning, everyone!" Her voice booms so everyone, even Miranda and I, can hear her. "This is a great human interest story, and it's going to air this evening at six o'clock. I'll need all of you to sign a release form. If any of you don't want to be on camera, you'll need to leave."

No one leaves.

"Great! Now, I'll just need you to do what you were doing—chanting and marching. Beth, I'll talk to you while they're all walking behind us and ask you some questions. Ready?"

Mom nods her head, waiting for the questions to

start. The cameraman uses his fingers to count down from three, then he points at Cynthia. That is her cue to begin.

"We're here today in the parking lot of an Urgent Care center in Richardson. I'm speaking with Beth Coleman, who is the organizer of the protest that you see behind me. A group of concerned parents is marching and chanting the words, 'Our Children, Our Choice.' Beth, you told me that one of the doctors here vaccinated your daughter against your wishes. Is that correct?"

"Yes, that's right." Mom seems nervous. She doesn't know if she should look at the camera, or at Cynthia.

"When did that happen?" the reporter asks.

"On Saturday. My daughter wanted to be vaccinated and I told her no, because I think they're dangerous. She went behind my back and convinced the doctor to do it anyway. That's completely illegal. He's not allowed to do that without my consent." She's speaking more confidently now.

"Would you say that you're part of the anti-vaxx movement that is becoming more prevalent across the country?"

"Oh, yes, I'm completely against all vaccinations," replies Mom. She gestures to the group behind her. "We all are. We believe they are poisonous and cause many more problems than they prevent. As parents, we should have the right to choose whether or not to vaccinate our children."

"But your daughter wanted to make that choice for herself, is that right?" asks Cynthia.

"Well, yes, but she's a minor. She's only sixteen, and the doctor cannot do that without parental consent. What he did is illegal."

"So, if your daughter was eighteen, of legal age, then you would be okay with it?"

"Uh, well, uh…" I could hear Mom stutter while she's trying to figure out the best way to answer this question. I know it will never be okay with her, no matter how old I am.

"Well, I would hope," she begins, "that my daughter would make smart decisions, based on the things I taught her as I was raising her."

"And what about the doctor who vaccinated her without your consent? What do you think should happen to him?"

She gets a very determined look on her face, and I see her small hands clench into fists.

"I will make sure he loses his medical license! I've already called a malpractice lawyer. He will NOT get away with this."

Cynthia turns her focus back to the camera and says cheerfully, "Thank you, Beth Coleman and her fellow protestors. I'm Cynthia Mitchell with WRIC Channel 11."

They start packing up, and I hear Cynthia tell my mom that they may or may not use the entire film. The van rolls away, and Mom and the marchers get back to business.

I need to call Dr. Tyrell. This can't be good for him at all. From what I can see, the protestors aren't going to let anyone get passed them. So, they aren't going to have much business today. But, honestly, how long can my mom and her crew hang out here? Will it be half a day? Or, maybe all day? I have no way of knowing.

I dig around in my backpack, knowing that his business card is in there somewhere. Finally, under the lip gloss and two phone chargers, I find it. I enter the numbers into my phone and hear it ring—three, then four times. Then voicemail. No! I really need to talk to him.

I hit the redial button, and it still goes straight to voicemail. I redial five times, until he finally picks up.

"This is Dr. Tyrell." He sounds so depressed as he answers. Hearing his voice, I feel terrible. This whole mess is all my fault. If I hadn't convinced him to vaccinate me, my mom and her friends wouldn't be marching in front of his Urgent Care center. And they wouldn't have called the news. And, did my mom say that she called an attorney? Oh, god, I shouldn't have called. I'm sure I'm the last person in the world he wants to talk to.

"This is Dr. Tyrell—who's this?"

"It's—it's Cassidy Coleman."

I hear him breathe deeply, then let out a big sigh.

"Dr. Tyrell," I began. "I'm so sorry! I— "

But he interrupts me before I can speak another word.

"It's not your fault, Cassidy. I'm not mad at you. I knew what I was doing and what the potential consequences were. Now I have to live with those consequences."

He chuckles.

"Your mom moves fast—I've already had a call from the Medical Review Board. They want me to come in for a hearing in a couple of weeks."

"A hearing?" I ask. "What does that mean?"

"Well, they'll decide if there will be any disciplinary measures taken against me."

"Like what?"

"It could range from my not practicing medicine

for a while, to losing my medical license forever."

Forever? That's ridiculous!

"I want to help you," I tell him. "What can I do to help?"

"Cassidy, there's nothing you can do. I need to handle this my-" He stops talking right in the middle of a word.

"Actually, I think there is a way you can help me. How would you feel about testifying on my behalf at the hearing? You could explain to the Board why you felt so strongly about being vaccinated."

This sounds like a good idea. I would love to fix this mess for Dr. Tyrell if I can. He has been nothing but helpful, ever since that first day he saw Angie and diagnosed her leukemia.

"Yes!" I say emphatically. "Let me know where and when, and I'll be there."

"Okay, good! Thank you, Cassidy. It means a lot to me. I'll be in touch with the details."

Chapter Twenty-Three

When Dr. Tyrell hangs up the phone, I just stare at it for a long moment. Then I turn my head to look at Miranda.

"Wow!" Her eyes are as big as saucers. "This is amazing! What have you gotten yourself into?"

I shift into drive and tell her, "I'll fill you in on the way to school."

We are so late—if we're lucky, we'll make it to school before second period starts. I tell Miranda the whole story.

"You feel really strongly about this, don't you?" she asks me. Her voice has a serious tone I haven't heard before.

"Of course I do. Angie would still be alive if it wasn't for me."

"Yeah. I get that. Even though it wasn't your fault." She gives me some serious side-eye, along with a small smile.

"Mmm hmm…it didn't happen to you, Miranda. You might feel differently if it did." I feel my eyes fill with tears again. "I miss her every single day. And I can't get rid of this guilt that I'm feeling. But now I have the opportunity to possibly help Dr. Tyrell. I'm just not sure what to do for him. And I know that anything I do to help him will piss off my mom. Ugh!" I bang the steering wheel with both hands. "I'm stuck in the middle of an impossible situation."

Miranda is applying a cotton candy shade of lipstick, checking herself out in the visor mirror. The color matches her fluffy sweater perfectly.

I pull away from the Urgent Care. Good thing school is only ten minutes away.

"You should talk to Ms. Malone about this—she would go nuts about it. She loves true crime."

I chuckle at that.

"True crime? Is that what this is?"

"Close enough!" She puts her lipstick in her bag and winks at me.

Since we get to school late, we have to park way off in the west lot, affectionately known as BFE. We run across the parking lot, dodging between the newer Honda Civics and a few classic VW Bugs and Camaros. The gearheads like to restore old cars and most of the time they turn out great.

We check in at the office and are given tardy slips by the school administrator, Mrs. Thomas. She's a total sweetheart, who really hates handing out the slips. Three tardies mean an automatic detention and it breaks her heart to give someone a detention slip. I've seen her cry because of it.

"Girls, please try hard to be on time. You know I

hate doing this. I'd much rather check you out because of a dentist appointment, but I can't stand it when you're late." Her eyes are misting already.

I spend the morning trying to get caught up on the work I missed. There's a lot. But I'm lucky, and my teachers let me spend a lot of the class time working on those assignments.

At lunch, instead of going to the cafeteria, I decide to check in with Ms. Malone. The door to her room is closed—I knock gently and hear her mumble, "Come in."

She's at her desk reading and eating a sandwich. When she sees me she jumps up and hurries around her desk. Before I know it, she grabs me in a huge hug.

"Oh, Cassidy, it feels like I haven't seen you in forever!"

I hug her back—it finally feels like my normal is coming back to me. Being in this classroom with this teacher feels so good. I have spent the last couple of weeks in a haze—nothing is the way it is supposed to be.

She pulls away from me and asks, "How are you, honey?"

That does it. The floodgates open and before I know it, I'm sobbing. She leads me to the cute little blue loveseat in the corner and we just sit there for a few minutes. She hands me a tissue box and just lets me cry. When the tears finally stop, I start to tell her the whole story. She knows about Angie's leukemia, of course, so I start from Thanksgiving—when I gave her the measles.

"So now you're going to testify at this hearing for Dr. Tyrell?" Ms. Malone asks me.

"I want to. I really want to help him. I know that

my mom won't like it, but I feel like this whole vaccine issue is bigger than my mother and me. We can still love each other and have a good relationship, but I really need to do what I think is right."

"I think that's the right attitude to have, honey. And I think if you tell your mom exactly what you told me, she'll understand."

"I hope so. Hey, do you think you can help me kind of prepare for this hearing? I have no idea what to expect."

"Sure, if I can! I don't know what to expect, either, but we can do a bunch of research on different state laws around the country."

Different laws? That's news to me.

"They're not all the same? How do you know that different states have different laws?" I ask her.

"There have been stories on the news over the years that I've seen. I never paid much attention, but we should definitely dig in and find out about them. That could have an impact on Dr. Tyrell's hearing. Do you know what could potentially happen to him?"

"He told me that it could be anywhere from not being able to practice medicine for a few weeks to completely losing his license."

"Hmmm…or, maybe nothing would happen," says Ms. Malone, thoughtfully. "That's the outcome we want."

"Do you think that's possible?" I ask.

"I think it is if you are prepared, and if you do your homework on this topic. Come see me after school and we can get started."

I spend the rest of the day getting assignments that I've missed and trying my best to get caught up in each of my classes. Honestly, it isn't as bad as I thought it would be. We're in that weird time between Thanksgiving and Winter Break, where time slows down a bit. Sure, we're getting ready for finals, but there isn't a whole lot of new material that I need to learn.

I know that I need to spend time on my schoolwork, and I will, but as soon as that last bell rings, I head toward Ms. Malone's room.

I open the door and see her sitting at her desk, engrossed in whatever is on her laptop. She doesn't notice me enter the room until I close the door behind me.

"Oh, hey, I'm glad you're here!" she says, as she looks up from her computer. "I think I've found some good stuff."

I pull a chair close to hers and look at the screen where she's pointing to a website loaded on her computer. On the desk next to the laptop I notice a spiral notebook sitting wide open. Ms. Malone has been taking a lot of notes—several pages are covered with her neat handwriting. I can make out some of the words, like "herd immunity" and "consent." It looks like she has been doing a lot of research.

"Check this out," she says, drawing my attention to the screen. "I think we're on to something. So, your mom is upset because Dr. Tyrell immunized you without her consent, right?"

"Right."

"This is really interesting. There have actually been situations where a parent is not present when a child is vaccinated! This happens during school vaccination events. Sometimes, the vaccination clinic comes to the school to immunize a lot of kids at once." She pauses and leans back in her chair.

"This could be really helpful," she says, mostly to herself. "These vaccination clinics wouldn't happen here at the high school, because all of the kids here would have already gotten all the shots. But I bet they do them at the elementary school."

That makes sense to me.

"Do you know anyone that works at an elementary school?" I ask her.

She turns to me and grins.

"As a matter of fact, I do. The school nurse at Crape Myrtle Elementary is one of my best friends."

"Oh, I know where that is!" I exclaim. "I didn't go there, but it's in my neighborhood."

"Let's give her a call and see what she has to say about these in-school vaccination clinics."

Ms. Malone takes her iPhone from her purse and quickly dials the number labeled "Jenni." She puts the phone on speaker, so I can also hear the conversation. Jenni answers on the second ring.

"Hey, girl!" she answers in a sing-song voice. "Is it wine o'clock already?"

Ms. Malone chuckles—she sounds a little embarrassed.

"No, I'm actually here with a student and we have a couple questions for you."

"Oh! I see. I'm happy to help you if I can." Jenni sounds completely different—she put on her professional voice. "What can I do for you?"

"So, Cassidy Coleman and I are working on a project together. It has to do with school vaccination clinics. Have you ever had them at your school?"

"Oh, sure, all the time. Especially in the fall, before flu season really kicks in."

"How do you handle parents that don't want their

children to be vaccinated?" Ms. Malone asks.

"Well, we send home information fliers twice a week for four weeks before the clinic, because we want to make sure all of the parents are aware. If they don't want their kids to receive the shot for any reason, it's their responsibility to let us know. Otherwise, they will receive it. And, you know this, it's best for everyone for these kids to be immunized against the flu. The egg allergy isn't even a thing anymore."

Egg allergy? What is she talking about? Ms. Malone must have seen the confused expression on my face, because she asks her friend to explain.

"Some flu vaccines contain egg protein, so if a person is allergic to eggs they might have a reaction to the vaccine. But, there are vaccines now that don't contain that protein, so we just use them. I've never seen a kid have a reaction to a flu shot in the nine years I've been working here."

Ms. Malone makes notes in her notebook, which is quickly running out of room.

"Is there anything else I can help you ladies with?" asks Jennifer.

"No, this is great!" replies Ms. Malone. "I'll call you later. Thanks so much!"

"Any time—bye, bye!"

"That has to help Dr. Tyrell."

"I agree. So, now we have data that proves parents don't always have to give their consent in order for a child to receive a vaccination. My guess is that most of the time it's good to have their consent, but it doesn't seem to stand in the way every single time." She looks at me and smiles. "That's a really good precedent."

Ms. Malone clicks on another browser tab and begins explaining again.

"Look at this—there are fifteen states that legally allow minors to be vaccinated without parental consent. And in Alaska, children of any age can consent to any type of healthcare."

I sit back in my chair, confused. I find it difficult to believe that there are states that allow teens to make all these decisions, and here I am trying to keep a really good doctor from possibly losing his medical license. If I just lived in a different state, all of this could have been avoided. Angie might even still be alive.

But I can't think like that. I know that I should only worry about the things that I can control. Right now, that means helping Dr. Tyrell.

"Fifteen states—why isn't Texas one of them?" I wonder aloud.

"I don't know, but maybe we can help change that. At least, maybe we can help Dr. Tyrell and make sure nothing bad happens to him."

Chapter Twenty-Four

I don't have to wait long to hear from Dr. Tyrell about the hearing. The date is set for December 21, which is about two weeks after Ms. Malone and I found the information about vaccination clinics in schools and the laws in different states. She offered to come along for what she called "moral support," but I think she really wants to be there to see how it'll all pan out. She's invested now.

I've been spending my time between both of my parents' homes. I was sick and tired of having to choose between them, so I decided not to. Dad called a Family Law attorney who said that at my age, it's really better if everyone can just work things out. That's what most divorced couples with teenagers do. This makes sense to me.

I bring enough clothing and toiletries to my dad's to make sure that I will never need to pack a separate bag if I want to go over on the spur of the moment. My favorite pictures of Angie and me hang on the walls of my bedroom at both houses. Dollar Tree has a new selection of fairy lights, especially since it's the holiday season. This way, I can decorate both rooms so they're practically identical.

The biggest difference between the two rooms is not how they're decorated or how they look—it's how they feel. At Dad's house, there's a constant feeling of stability. Dad is predictable. I know that when I see him, he'll be wearing jeans and a t-shirt. He doesn't have to dress up when he works from home.

The days that I stay with Dad, I usually swing by Kroger to pick up something easy to make for dinner. They have a whole selection of ready-to-cook meals. My favorite is the beef bulgogi—thin slices of beef and onion, marinated in a tangy Korean sauce. All I have to do is cook it in one of the cast-iron skillets hanging from the pot rack in the kitchen, and it's ready in a flash. A little rice in the rice cooker completes the meal. I'm proud of my new culinary abilities.

At dinner we'd talk about everyday things: school, Christmas coming up, even current events. Dad's really well-informed about everything going on in the world. If there's anything in the news that I'm not sure about, he can explain it to me and help me understand. Like, there's a newly discovered respiratory virus that was discovered in China. It seems to be spreading pretty rapidly over there, but he doesn't think it's anything we need to worry about.

We go running together, too, which I desperately need. I missed the end of the fall track season, which includes the State Finals. I'm trying to stay in decent shape for the spring season, so I'll get in a few miles with Dad whenever he's up for it.

I'll spend a couple of days at Dad's and then I'll start missing Mom. I started going back to her house shortly after Ms. Malone and I began working on our strategy for the hearing together. I just missed her. I was tired of being mad at her, and I just wanted to be with her again.

At Mom's house, my senses wake up. Smell and taste are always well taken care of there. When I walk in the front door after school, I never know what will be cooking but most of the time it's exotic and delicious. One day it would be Chicken Tikka Masala, and the next she'd be baking a veggie lasagna. She had recently started cooking with meat a little more. That's a big step for her, and I appreciate it.

Mom has always been pretty stuck in her ways. For her to make a change like this is a big deal.

We haven't talked about the hearing or my getting vaccinated. I know that I'll have to go back for the second round of shots in a while—I really hope that won't be a problem. My game plan is to wait and see what happens at the hearing, and then figure out the best way to proceed. If Dad needs to get a lawyer to help me move forward, I know that he will. But I really don't want to screw up my relationship with Mom.

Things between us are getting so much better— our relationship is almost back to the way it was before. We're talking and laughing again, mostly about small, unimportant things. I still don't feel able to talk to her about Angie's death and how I feel about it. I'm not sure she's ready to hear me, and I just don't want to fight with her.

I have my pro-vaxx team that I can confide in when I need to. That is Dad, Ms. Malone, and Miranda.

They'll all be with me at the hearing, mostly for moral support. Ms. Malone will be available with all kinds of supporting data, mostly about vaccine laws in other states.

As it happens with most news stories, the headline about my mom protesting at the Urgent Care dies down. I'm very happy to learn that Dr. Tyrell was given permission to continue working up to the date of the hearing—he just has to make sure he doesn't treat any minors without their parents' consent.

One evening about a week before the hearing Mom and I are in her kitchen making dinner. She's placing the fixings for shrimp and veggie spring rolls on top of rice paper, and I'm working on the fried rice.

She surprises me when she asks, "Are you ready for next week?"

Since we haven't discussed the hearing at all, I'm not sure what she's talking about. "Next week?" I ask.

"The hearing, Cass." She's artistically placing julienned strips of cucumber, carrots, and radish in the middle of the transparent wrapper. On top of that she places whole basil leaves and a pink, cooked shrimp.

"Oh, um, yeah, I think so." I'm not sure how much I should say. She's my mom, but we're on opposite sides when it comes to the hearing.

"You're going to testify on the doctor's behalf, right?"

I'm afraid to meet her eyes. I look at the rice and celery cooking in the skillet and just say, "Yeah."

"Okay," she replies. "It's probably time to make room in the middle of the skillet for the eggs."

And that is all she says. We set up the TV trays in the family room because we want to watch an episode of our favorite show, *The Good Place*. We're desperately behind—the whole series ended months ago. But Mom and I promised each other that we would only watch it together. It's our thing.

Mom and I prepared a pretty amazing dinner—the fried rice I made is full of crunchy veggies, and it isn't too salty. Sometimes I overdo it a bit with the soy sauce. I need to learn that more isn't always better. And I scrambled the eggs just right.

The shrimp and basil spring rolls are to die for. Mom made a peanut dipping sauce that has a bit of sriracha. Now that I'm spending a good bit of time with Mom again, I really want to learn how to cook all of the delicious and different foods she makes. Dad is the best steak griller, I know, and he does fine with chicken and spaghetti, but he isn't all that creative.

On the television we're watching Kristen Bell and her crew at a party—everyone is happy and chatty, and they're talking to different people from throughout history. One guy says something, and I don't think I heard it correctly. I look at Mom, and she has a real pissed off look on her face.

I grab the remote and back up about a minute so I can hear it again. Mom reaches out to grab it from me, but I tell her, "I just want to hear what he said. I didn't hear it."

It's a guy from ancient Phoenicia who's speaking. He died young from a cut on his hand. He said, "I would've killed for a vaccine. Any vaccine. It's crazy that you guys just don't like them now."

I lose it. I am laughing so hard that my sides began to ache. The timing of this joke on our favorite show is remarkable. Mom doesn't find the incident as funny as I do, but I still cannot stop laughing.

"Mom, come on," I say as I try to recover my

breath. "That's funny. It's like fate. And it's funny."

She takes a bite of her spring roll. "Well," she says as she smiles at me. "I suppose it was a little funny. He just wanted *any* vaccine." And she giggles.

"Right?? He didn't care what kind, he just wanted one. We should take him to see Dr. Tyrell."

Mom starts laughing so hard, she has to cover her mouth with her hand so she won't spew her shrimp onto the TV tray.

Chapter Twenty-Five

Christmas falls on a Friday this year, so the Texas Medical Board hearing takes place during my winter break. I have absolutely no idea what to expect—I just know that Dad, Ms. Malone, Miranda, and I are piling into Dad's Subaru and going to a meeting in downtown Dallas. Well, actually, Dad said it's off of I35 and Medical District Drive, in one of the hospitals.

I was expecting a big courtroom scene like they show on TV, but I suppose it makes more sense.

Mom will be driving and sitting with her lawyer.

The night before, Miranda and I coordinated our outfits for today. We agree that we want to appear as mature and professional as possible. I plan to wear a black knee-length skirt, with a cute pink sweater. I've always loved black and pink together. I actually blow-dry my hair this morning, which really took a lot of effort. I prefer my no-nonsense ponytail.

Miranda is going to wear a short-sleeve, V-neck navy blue dress that falls just above her knees and these awesome black boots she found at Goodwill.

Dad and I first drive by Miranda's house to pick her up and then go to Ms. Malone's. When we pull up into her driveway, I climb out of the car so Ms. Malone can sit in the passenger seat. I climb in the back with Miranda.

It is a beautiful day for late December. The temperature is in the mid-fifties but it feels warmer because the sun is so bright.

"How long will it take to get there, Dad?" I ask.

"Oh, around thirty to forty-five minutes. Traffic should be a breeze this week, so close to the holiday."

Dad maneuvers the Subaru onto westbound 635. In the passenger seat, Ms. Malone takes a tablet out of her bag and turns on the screen.

"I've made some notes, and I thought it might be a good idea for us to strategize a bit before the meeting today."

"Do you think we're all going to have to speak?" asks Miranda. I know that she's just expecting to observe and provide moral support.

"Oh, no, honey, I wasn't thinking that at all. This is just the first time we've all been together, so I thought it would be a good idea to go over some of the data that I've found."

"I have notes, too," I announce, leaning forward to be able to see Ms. Malone a little better. "I printed out that information about the vaccine laws in different states."

"That's good to have handy. I do think they're mostly going to want to hear your personal story.

They'll want to know why you're so passionate about being vaccinated and how Angie's illness and death affected you. Just speak from your heart, honey."

Dad's right—it takes just over half an hour to arrive at the hospital. I'm surprised to notice that it's right next door to the Children's Hospital where I had spent so much time with Angie. It looks like there's even a sky bridge that connects them. I point it out to Dad.

"They're affiliated with each other," he tells me. "The doctors at both hospitals work together, especially when it involves researching new treatments."

As we drive past, I stare at the big red balloon on the side of the Children's hospital. I feel a rush of emotions—sadness at the loss of my friend and longing for the time when she was still alive and I still had hope that she'd walk out of that building. I turn away, facing the future instead of the past.

Dad pulls into the covered parking garage and pushes a button that ejects a ticket. The garage is crammed with cars – we keep driving up, searching for a spot and not finding one. Finally, we find a few open spots on the top-most level.

We all make our way from the car to the bank of elevators. Ms. Malone stuffs her tablet into her huge purse as we walk. The doors to an elevator open as we walk up and step inside, following a trio of nurses. They are wearing bright, colorful scrubs and are all laughing and talking animatedly. As we step into the elevator, one of them smiles at us and asks, "Which floor?" as she holds her finger over the numbered buttons.

Dad looks back at her with a confused look on his face.

"Dad, don't you know where we're going?" I ask. I'm getting a little nervous—I would have thought he knew exactly where we need to go.

"Um….it's a conference room on the first floor," he says hesitantly.

"Oh, okay," says the nurse. "Then you need to start at the hospital lobby. Make sure you check in at the security desk. They'll point you in the right direction." And her fingers push the right button.

"Thank you. I appreciate your help," says Dad. He's always over-the-top polite. I think it's kinda cute. My dad is nice to everyone.

As we make our way through the hospital lobby and toward the security desk, I notice how different it is from the Children's hospital. There are no butterflies hanging from the ceiling or twinkling LED lights that mimic stars. This is just what you would expect from a hospital that cares for adults; it's stark, white, and sterile.

The one thing that is similar is the security desk. They still want to make sure that anyone who visits this hospital is supposed to be here. We stand in the short line, then present our IDs when it's our turn.

The concierge is speaking to Dad, and I see her point down the hallway and indicate to the right. Dad thanks her politely, of course, and he motions us to follow him.

We pass the main elevator bank where most people seem to be going. A few continue down the hallway like we do. There is a large sign that reads "Radiology," and the waiting room is full. Those people are probably getting an x-ray, or maybe a CT scan.

I make eye contact with an old man sitting on a chair that looks like it could have been in someone's living room. It is dark blue and very comfy looking. He is watching our little group as we pass by—he is wearing a long-sleeved t-shirt and sweatpants. It makes sense, I suppose, to dress comfortably when you have to wait for hours in the hospital. He has a great mop of white hair on his head. Apparently, baldness doesn't run in his family.

When our eyes meet, his mouth curves into a smile and he nods at me. I smile and nod back.

"Cassidy, come on!" I hear Dad call to me. Oops— I got distracted and I'm lagging behind. I jog a bit to catch up, just as they turn right down a short hallway. Dad stops in front of a closed door. There's a sign that reads, "Bluebonnet Room."

"I'm pretty sure this is it," he says, and he pulls the door open.

The room contains the largest conference table I've ever seen. Thirty people can easily sit around it. On one wall an equally large television is mounted. It must measure at least 75 inches. There are no windows—just bright lights installed in the ceiling.

We aren't the first to arrive. Dr. Tyrell is already seated at the table, next to a man who must be his attorney. Across from him sits a woman—wait a minute. It's Mom! But I don't recognize her at first because she is dressed in a way that I've never seen before. Her hair is smooth and knotted at the back of her neck in a neat bun. She is wearing a beige suit with a crisp white blouse that I also haven't seen before. She looks like a completely different person.

On the television screen a woman appears. There is also a man sitting at what would be considered the head of the table. Everyone has papers and a notepad in front of them. Of course, they all turn and look at us as we enter—awkward!

"Are we late?" asks Miranda.

"Not at all! We're all a bit early," answers the man at the head of the table. He stands as he speaks. I guess that he's around 40 years old. He's tall, with dark skin and hair that is cut very short. He wears wire-rimmed glasses.

"I'm Dr. Henderson," he continues. "And joining us from Austin is Dr. Abbott." He gestures toward the blonde woman on the screen, who gives us a quick wave. "Which one of you is the young lady who visited Dr. Tyrell?"

"That's me. I'm Cassidy." My voice comes out in almost a whisper, and I clear my throat. Dr. Henderson chuckles.

"No need to be nervous, Cassidy, this won't hurt a bit. We're just here to have a conversation. Why don't you all take a seat? Cassidy, sit next to me if you don't mind."

He holds out the chair closest to him, as Dad, Ms. Malone, and Miranda take their places around the table. Ms. Malone sits next to Dr. Tyrell, and they smile at each other.

Dr. Henderson sits in his chair and addresses everyone at the table.

"Let me explain this process to all of you. Beth Coleman has filed a complaint against Dr. Tyrell for practicing medicine on her daughter, Cassidy, without her consent. We are here to see if that complaint is valid, and if there will be disciplinary actions taken against Dr. Tyrell. Dr. Abbott and I are both members in good standing of the Texas Medical Board. This case has already been through several preliminary phases, and we are now at the Informal Settlement Conference. We are hoping to reach a resolution today, which I believe we will. Over ninety percent of complaints that the Board receives are resolved at this phase."

"Dr. Henderson, which phases have already been completed?" This question comes from Ms. Malone, who is busily taking notes. I think she's writing down everything the doctor says, word-for-word.

"So far, the Board has conducted a preliminary evaluation and a thorough investigation. Today, we are hoping that everyone can agree on a solution. We definitely want to hear from all parties involved."

Ms. Malone nods as she scribbles.

Dr. Henderson turns to look at me directly. "Cassidy, I'd like to hear your story. Tell me what happened."

I pause for a moment to collect my thoughts. I want to tell my story and Angie's story, in a way that will be clear and honest. I want to honor Angie.

"Angie was my best friend," I begin. "We had always done everything together. We were like sisters."

I glance around the table—everyone is looking at me, taking in my words. It feels good to share this with all the people here: my family, my friends, and these doctors. I want all of them to know about her. Miranda smiles and nods at me encouragingly.

"We were on the track team together, and she was the best—the star. She would have gotten a full ride to some college. She was that good. But then on that day in the fall, I noticed bruising on the back of her legs. I took her to Urgent Care. That was the first time we met Dr. Tyrell. And he said that she needed to go to the Emergency Room, because he was pretty sure she had leukemia. I called her mom first, and then I drove her to the hospital. They started treatment pretty much right away. Well, first they did that thing where they tried to remove as many of the cancer cells from her blood as possible. I don't remember what it's called."

"Pheresis," says Dr. Henderson.

"Right, that's it. Pheresis. But they tried a month of chemo, and then they said it wasn't working. They needed to go to Plan B. And she had to wait in the hospital until her new cells would be ready. This was in November, and we always had Thanksgiving together. Since she couldn't be at our table with us, I brought a bunch of food to the hospital. On Thanksgiving Day I wasn't feeling bad. My throat was just a bit scratchy, but that was it. It never occurred to me that I was getting sick. Never."

I pause for a moment, gathering my thoughts. It isn't nearly as difficult to talk about as I had anticipated. Talking about what happened actually feels empowering—like I'm able to do a small thing for Angie.

I notice a bottle of water on the table in front of me. I remove the cap and take a few sips. That's better. I'm ready to continue.

"We were watching the *Home Alone* movies. One of the Child Life ladies had brought the DVDs to us. I had pulled the chair right next to the bed, so we could share the piece of apple pie."

"So, you were really close to each other, right?" asks Dr. Henderson.

"Right. I spent the night on the couch in her room, and when I woke up I felt horrible. And I felt guilty for being there. I picked up my backpack and got out of there as quickly as I could. I didn't even wake her up to say good-bye. I went to Mom's and just crashed. All I wanted was my bed. And then Dad got me and took me to Urgent Care."

"And that was when Dr. Tyrell diagnosed you with the measles?" he asks.

"Yes."

He turns toward Dr. Tyrell and asks, "What course of treatment did you recommend for Cassidy?"

"I told her father to treat the symptoms—the fever, rash, and cough. If she demonstrated any difficulty breathing, or other respiratory distress, then he should take her to an Emergency Room immediately."

"Okay. That sounds like proper advice. Dr. Abbott," he continues, addressing the TV screen, "do you have any questions?"

The woman on the television clears her throat before she begins. "I don't have any questions regarding Dr. Tyrell's treatment or his recommendations. That's exactly how the measles should be treated. I'd like to know why this young woman caught this disease in the first place. Why wasn't she vaccinated?"

Mom looks at her attorney, as if asking what she should say. He nods at her and nudges a pad of paper in front of her. It must have been filled with notes for her, so she would say the right thing.

She looks at Dr. Abbott and says, "I have never believed that vaccines were necessary, or good for people. Especially for children. I think they're full of chemicals that are potentially toxic and dangerous."

"What qualifies you to make that decision?" asks Dr. Abbott.

"Well, there's a lot of information on the Internet that shows how dangerous they are. And the package inserts explain what they contain. None of those ingredients sound safe to me."

Mom's lawyer decides to chime in at that time. "I understand that there is a debate as to whether or not vaccines are safe," he begins. But Dr. Abbott interrupts him.

"Debates involve differences in opinion. There are no differences in opinion when something is a scientific fact. Vaccines are safe and effective, period."

The lawyer speaks again. "This isn't our topic of discussion today. The fact is that Ms. Coleman has the right to make all decisions regarding her daughter's medical care. Dr. Tyrell administered the vaccination without her consent. And Cassidy Coleman is a minor child who is not yet capable of making those decisions for herself."

"Hey!" I exclaim. I am insulted! Who does this jerk think he is? "You think that as soon as I turn eighteen, I'll magically know what's best for me? Because of what I went through, which includes the death of my best friend, I think I have a pretty good idea already."

"Now, now," says Dr. Henderson, trying to calm everyone down. "Let's all take a breath. This topic is a difficult one, and it stirs up lots of emotions. We are here to examine the facts. Let's do that. Cassidy, please continue with your story."

I nod. He's right, I know that. I'm here to help Dr. Tyrell, and that's what I intend to do.

"I'm finally starting to feel better and thinking about going back to school, and that's when Angie's mom called me. She told me that Angie died from having the measles. My best friend died because I gave her an illness that could have been prevented."

I pause and look at the people in the conference room. All eyes are on me.

"After the funeral, I went to Angie's house and saw

her parents. I went by myself. Dad came to the funeral with me, but I just wanted to be on my own for a while afterwards. Angie's parents were wonderful to me. I thought they'd blame me, but they didn't. We talked, and I got some salsa verde to take home. But after I left I felt like I had to do something—I didn't want what happened to Angie to happen to anyone else. That's when I went to the Urgent Care and convinced Dr. Tyrell to vaccinate me for the other diseases that I should have already been vaccinated for."

Dr. Henderson makes a few notes on the paper in front of him. Then he shifts to look at Dr. Tyrell.

"Okay, Doctor—you know the rules. Cassidy is sixteen, and she didn't have parental consent. What caused you to do what she asked?"

"Well, you're right. I know the rules. But Cassidy gave a very compelling argument. And, like Dr. Abbott, I know the science behind vaccinations. I know that while they could potentially harm a patient who is allergic to one of the ingredients, vaccines are safe and effective for the vast majority of people. I also know that there are quite a few states that already allow teenagers who are Cassidy's age, and sometimes even younger, to make this decision for themselves."

"I'm glad you brought that up," interjects Dr. Abbott. "A bill has been introduced to the Texas State Legislature that would lower the age of consent for vaccinations to sixteen. So we might be joining those other states soon."

Dr. Henderson is nodding. "That's right. And, honestly, I think because of that fact, and because this young lady explained her rationale very well, I've decided that there should not be any disciplinary action taken against Dr. Tyrell. Dr. Abbott, do you agree?"

"One hundred percent."

Mom and her attorney are whispering to each other—I can't hear what they're saying. Dr. Tyrell just looks relieved. I feel like a weight has been lifted from my shoulders. But then something occurs to me.

"Um, I have a question."

"What's that, Cassidy?" asks Dr. Henderson.

"Dr. Tyrell told me that I'll need to have a second round of shots. Can I get those?"

Dr. Henderson looks at Mom—he doesn't say anything, just looks at her. Her attorney whispers something in her ear.

She clears her throat before she says, "Yes, that's fine."

Dr. Henderson slides a piece of paper over to her across the table.

"Great," he says. "Please sign this consent form."

And she does. She slides the paper back to Dr. Henderson. I see her pretty, loopy signature as the paper breezes past me.

Dr. Henderson inspects it, then states with authority, "Folks, I think we can call it a day. We have a successful resolution regarding this complaint. And Cassidy can receive the next round of her vaccinations. Are there any questions?"

There aren't.

Chapter Twenty-Six

Eight Years Later

I bump up the speed of the treadmill to 6.5 miles per hour. I have about three minutes left, and I want to finish strong. The Bolder Boulder is coming up in about a month, and I really want to have a good race. A 10K isn't tough for me, but I'm not as young as I used to be. So, training is a must.

I need to take a quick shower before my 1:15 meeting. It's 12:45—I have plenty of time. I love having a fitness center on site at the hospital—it makes getting a run in during my day so much easier. And these Colorado winters are no joke. I'm not always able to run outside and, honestly, I'm still not completely used to the cold. Some of my friends at work will go for a run when the temperature is in the single digits, but that does not sound like fun to me. I'll stick to the treadmill.

I have lived in Denver for about a year, working for the University of Colorado Hospital in north Denver. I work closely with medical staff on end-of-life issues, organ transplant cases, and sexual boundaries among staff and patients. There's a lot involved in Healthcare Ethics.

A few days after Dr. Tyrell's hearing I received a phone call from Dr. Henderson. He told me that I had been on his mind since the hearing, and he wanted to run something by me. The hospital was starting a new program to introduce high school students to various aspects of the medical field and hospital administration. Because of my passion regarding vaccinations and my effort in assisting Dr. Tyrell, he thought I'd be a good fit for the Healthcare Ethics program. He was right.

I spent six months shadowing Marcia, the Healthcare Ethicist. We visited patients who were at the end of their lives and talked to them about the best way to make them comfortable. Marcia was involved with decisions that had to be made when a young woman was brought into the Emergency Department, after being hit head on by a drunk driver. Things didn't look good for her.

There had been a patient waiting for a new liver—she had been on the transplant list for many months and was in desperate need. The woman from the car accident was a match, and if she died would be the perfect donor. But she didn't have the little organ donor consent icon on her driver's license, and the hospital was having a hard time reaching her next of kin for permission. That's when Marcia stepped in and began discussing the ethics of using this liver for the patient who desperately needed it to save her life.

I sat in the corner like a fly on the wall, absorbing as much information as I could. It turned out that the car-accident woman was going through a divorce, and it took a while to reach her soon-to-be ex-husband. But at the time of the accident they were still married, and he was the one to make the decision about the liver. Working with Marcia through this very difficult issue was what caused me to realize that this is what I'm supposed to do with my life.

I spent the first two years of my higher education at a community college, and then I was lucky enough to win a small scholarship to the University of North Texas. I was able to "build my own major" because they didn't officially offer a bachelor's degree in Bioethics. Mom and Dad were both able to kick in some money to help. Mom had actually started a college fund for me years ago, and it had grown into a nice little nest egg—who knew?

Between doing some DoorDash work and living at home, I was able to graduate from college debt-free. Until I started my job in Colorado, I had no idea how strange that was. Everyone was talking about how many thousands of dollars in student loan debt they had. Who wants to start their working life like that? Rent in Denver is not cheap, and I know that a lot of people also have some pretty hefty car payments. I'm still driving Elsa. She's running great and we've been through a lot together. I bought her a set of all-season tires, and she has no problem in the snow.

When I decided to accept the job in Colorado, Mom and Dad were equally ambivalent. Sure, they were happy that I had a job offer right out of college, in the field that I majored in, but couldn't it be in

Texas? Luckily, they didn't push me too hard. After all, I was returning to their roots, wasn't I?

Anyway, Mom was busy managing the Angie Gutiérrez Memorial Scholarship, so I didn't think she'd have much time to miss me. It had been Miranda's idea; she was having great success with the foundation she began, in memory of her little brother. Even though he had been very small when he died, Miranda wanted the foundation to focus on what teens needed when they were diagnosed with cancer, and in the hospital for a long time. But, she soon discovered that it wasn't easy to say no to the younger patients. They all needed some distraction while they were stuck in the hospital.

Not surprisingly, since she was an organizational machine, she quickly raised a lot of money. I mean a lot—like, close to $100,000 in less than a year. She approached all the businesses in Richardson and asked for donations. When she wanted to reach out to businesses in neighboring cities, she convinced her parents to buy her a used car. It was all to honor the memory of her brother—they had to do it.

So, Miranda drove all over DFW in her forest-green Hyundai sedan. She had so much success with small and medium-sized businesses, that she wasn't at all nervous about asking the big guys for money. She visited AT&T, Cisco, and Toyota. She scheduled formal appointments and built PowerPoint presentations.

She even figured out how to get high school credit for the work she did for the foundation. It was incredible. An attorney donated her time to help form a 501c3 non-profit organization, and *Gifts From Luke* became official.

Her main focus was providing a tablet to every

patient on the cancer floor. Tablets are perfect for these kids because they can watch movies, call their friends, and play games. I would think that most of these kids would have one anyway, but Miranda explained how reality works, of course. So many of the families have monstrous medical bills and can't even think about buying a tablet for their child.

In addition to the tablets, *Gifts From Luke* is able to buy a ton of gift cards. The kids seem to like the Amazon cards the most, but they also like Target and Walmart. So when the kids are discharged from the hospital, they're able to go on a shopping spree. Mom helped Miranda with some of the administrative tasks, which lit a fire inside her—that's when she came to me with her idea. Mom wanted to start the Angie Gutiérrez Memorial Scholarship. Kids from all over Texas who were recovering from cancer and were ready to start college or a trade were eligible to apply.

I saw an energy in my mother that I had never seen before. She had a purpose now. It was amazing.

Mom helped me with my move. I didn't really have much, since I didn't have any furniture except what was in my childhood bedrooms at both Mom's and Dad's homes. I took the bed from Dad's and the dresser and desk from Mom's. Dad had an old loveseat for my living room, and Mom had a small dinette table and chairs for my kitchen. It looked like something snatched from a 1950s diner, and I loved it.

We rented a tiny trailer that Elsa was able to pull—it was just big enough to hold my meager belongings. We decided to turn the road trip into a mini-vacation. We stopped in Santa Fe for a couple of days, where we ate so much good food and drank the best margaritas in the world. Then we stopped in Colorado Springs to visit Pike's Peak and Garden of the Gods. We had the absolute best time together—it was like a reboot of our relationship.

I had rented the little apartment online because I had fallen in love with the pictures. The reviews of the property manager were mostly good, which helped. The apartment was half of a duplex in the older part of Denver. The streets were lined with huge trees and every single home was oozing with character.

My little slice of heaven was built in the 1950s. It was old and small and absolutely perfect for me. The hardwood floor was original and had been recently resurfaced and polished. I loved the crown molding and funky tile work in the kitchen and bathroom. Mom thought it was too old and that it would cause me nothing but trouble. Of course, I didn't care.

There was a small backyard that both residents of the duplex shared, but I had my own tiny patio. I found some gorgeous clay planters at a garage sale and planted some jalapeño and habanero peppers and a little bunch of cilantro. I really wanted to try and duplicate Angie's mom's salsa recipe.

We moved in quickly, because there was hardly anything to move, and Mom stuck around for a couple of days to help me set up. We found a decent set of dishes and pots and pans at Goodwill. On her last night with me we cooked together in my kitchen that wasn't big enough to accommodate two cooks. We made spaghetti and meatballs, which were *not* vegan. It was amazing!

The next day I drove Mom to DIA and said good-bye at passenger-drop-off. The drive home (it was so weird to say that!) was surreal. I parked Elsa in the driveway, beneath the carport. My apartment didn't have a garage, but I was okay with that. The carport would keep most of the snow off her in the winter. The back door that led into the kitchen was right next to the driveway, so it was super easy to get in the house; into my home.

Chapter Twenty-Seven

I finish my run and do some easy stretches, just to loosen up my calves a bit. After a quick shower I make my way to the conference room on the first floor. It accommodates 100 attendees, and it's a good thing that it does—every seat in the house is taken. Nurses, doctors, and medical students are equipped with some kind of recording device, either electronic or an old-fashioned pen and paper.

I'm surprised that with ten minutes to spare, the room is so packed. There are literally no empty spaces. People are standing in the back—hopefully, they won't mind standing for an hour.

I walk slowly toward the front of the room, scanning the faces. Most of them don't even seem to notice me. I set the laptop that I'm carrying on the podium and connect it to the projector. I turn to make sure that what's on my small screen is also displayed on the large screen behind me. I fire up the presentation, and then attach the lapel mic to the collar of my blouse. I tap it to make sure it's working.

"Good afternoon, everyone," I announce. The socializing stops immediately and I have their attention. "Welcome to today's presentation on Medical Ethics and Organ Transplants. I'm your Healthcare Ethics Specialist, Cassidy Coleman."

About the Author

Diane Windsor is an author and publisher in
Van Alstyne, Texas.

She's also a cancer mom. You never realize how many
families are faced with childhood cancer until you're
facing it, too.

Please take the time to leave a review of *Stuck* on
Goodreads and Amazon. Reviews are an author's
bread and butter!

Aunt Betty Wasn't Vaccinated

In the great "downsizing" of 2015, when we sold our house and began our "empty nester" years, I whittled away at my book collection. Many books were given away or sold. I kept only those that I felt a strong connection to. One of the books that I kept was, "Mrs. Mike, the Story of Katherine Mary Flannigan". I read it first in Middle School, and the story had a huge impact on me. It was the story of a New England girl who married a Canadian Mounted Policeman and ended up in the Northern Wilds of Canada. It was a tale of hardship and struggle, especially for someone who had never really known such concepts before.

What really stuck with me though, was that this young family lost all of their children in an epidemic, and like so many of that time period, ended up with a "second family" that was to give them some relief from the sorrow of children lost. This was before Jonas Salk and Marie Curie changed the world. This was before three strong generations of Americans who knew no real suffering from preventable childhood illnesses.

One of the only pictures I have ever seen of my Aunt Betty is of her lying serenely in her coffin. Aged 3, she succumbed to pertussis, commonly known as whooping cough. My grandparents lost two of seven children by the age of three. When Betty died, my grandmother was pregnant with her 6th child. It had been 8 years since her first-born son had died at 17 months. In addition to Betty, my grandparents had a 7 year old, 5 year old and an 8 month old in their home. And Betty and my 8 month old father were sick. Perilously so. There was so much concern that my 8 month old father would die on the night of August 28, 1935 that they held a prayer vigil for him, begging God to spare him, while quietly Betty took her last breath in the other room.

A now preventable childhood disease changed many lives that night. Aunt Betty died, and the suffering for my Grandparents was almost unbearable. How could God have taken one, while the other was being so dutifully covered with prayerful intercession? The story of his triumph against death, told many times as he grew up, gave my Dad both survivor's guilt and an obsession with being worthy of God's choosing him. So many lives affected by a single young death. A single death multiplied hundreds of times in the community that summer.

STUCK

One of the great ironies of the "anti-vaxxer" movement in the Western World has been that the people who fear vaccines for their children have no idea of the suffering of the people who lived before the relative childhood illness-free world they were raised in. They have no frame of reference for the consequences of trading one possible outcome (known, suspected and imagined vaccine side effects) for the certainty of another (life changing illness, disability and death from the preventable diseases). And unfortunately, the effects of preventable communicable or contagious illness are not isolated to a single person or family.

I truly feel for parents who believe, rightly or wrongly, that vaccines have caused their family harm. I also know that pharmaceutical companies can be greedy and are not to be trusted unquestioningly. But when I think of how many lives across entire communities are at risk (physically, emotionally and even spiritually) for each unvaccinated child who contracts measles, mumps, or pertussis, I realize these parents likely never had an Aunt Betty who they never had the chance to meet. They never had Grandparents who wistfully recounted stories of their children and neighborhoods being wiped out in the course of weeks. They never had a parent whose life was so changed by a dying sister that his gentle life of service was always tied to her passing.

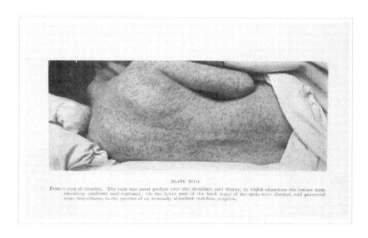

PLATE XCIII

Female case of measles. The rash was most profuse over the shoulders and thorax, in which situations the lesions were becoming confluent and engorged. On the lower part of the back many of the spots were checked and presented some resemblance to the papules of an unusually abundant papulose eruption.

I don't know how to console a grieving family who feels vaccines are dangerous and caused them harm. All I know is that not vaccinating those who are healthy and eligible risks a century of advances in preventable death. If we're afraid of the vaccines, let's work to fix that. Let's not reverse course! We owe this to ourselves, our children and future generations.

This blog post was written by Danita Zanrè about her father's sister. Reprinted with the author's permission.